YA
C

MY LIFE,
THE THEATER,
AND
OTHER
TRAGEDIES

A Novel by
Allen Zadoff

EGMONT
USA
NEW YORK

EGMONT
We bring stories to life

First published by Egmont USA, 2011
443 Park Avenue South, Suite 806
New York, NY 10016

1 3 5 7 9 8 6 4 2

www.egmontusa.com
www.allenzadoff.com

Library of Congress Cataloging-in-Publication Data
Zadoff, Allen.
My life, the theater, and other tragedies : a novel / by Allen Zadoff.
p.   cm.
Summary: While working backstage on a high school production of
"A Midsummer Night's Dream," sixteen-year-old Adam develops
feelings for a beautiful actress—which violates an unwritten code—
and begins to overcome the grief that has controlled him since his
father's death nearly two years earlier.
ISBN 978-1-60684-036-8 (hardcover) — ISBN 978-1-60684-256-0 (e-book)
[1. Theater—Fiction. 2. Interpersonal relations—Fiction.
3. Grief—Fiction. 4. High schools—Fiction. 5. Schools—Fiction.
6. New Jersey—Fiction.] I. Title.
PZ7.Z21My 2011 [Fic]—dc22 2010043619

Printed in the United States of America

CPSIA tracking label information:
Printed in March 2011 at Berryville Graphics, Berryville, Virginia

SPECIAL THANKS

Thanks to the theater people—actors, crew members, designers, directors, dramaturgs, producers, stage managers, and teachers—who have inspired me over the years. There are so many of you, I can't begin to name you all.

Present day I owe a very special thanks to the good folks at Egmont for their continued support. Doug Pocock, who gave my books a home, and Elizabeth Law, theater-lover-in-chief, who continues to be my editor, publisher, and supporter. Every author should be lucky enough to have a home like Egmont.

Thanks to the amazing SK Literary team—Shana Cohen, Jennifer Puglisi, and the brilliant and unflappable Stuart Krichevsky.

Thanks to Bobby Bowman, who took me to lunch at the right time and reminded me of lessons from Shakespeare.

Thanks to Pete Sauber, Technical Director at the Boston Court Performing Arts Center in Pasadena, who shared his technical expertise with me. Some of what he reads here will cause him (and techies everywhere) to turn pale and hyperventilate. There are technical details in the book that are imperfect, others with which I took dramatic license. If I made mistakes, know that I was doing my best to capture the spirit of technical theater and the amazing people who do it every day.

Those who wear black, I salute you.

"Are you sure
That we are awake?"

—WILLIAM SHAKESPEARE,
A Midsummer Night's Dream

SINCE NIGHT YOU LEFT ME.

I dream of my father.

It sneaks up on me in my sleep, this dream I have from time to time.

Maybe more than time to time. I think I have it every night, but most nights I sleep through and wake up in the morning having forgotten.

Some nights I'm not so lucky.

Tonight for instance.

My father is there with me one minute, the next minute gone, disappeared into the darkness. He's never dead in the dream. He's missing, which is much worse. At least with dead, you know what you're getting. But what is missing? Missing means he could be lost and need help. He could be hurt. He might have run away, abandoned me, Mom, and Josh. He might have been taken against his will.

If he's missing, he can still be found.

That's what's so painful about the dream. When I'm awake, I know my father is dead. He died in a car accident two years ago. A little less than two years. But in the dream, I don't know that. In the dream he's alive and I'm looking for him, searching everywhere with this giant wave of fear expanding in my chest.

Some nights I sleep through until morning, but not tonight. Tonight I'm in the middle of the dream when my eyes pop open. I reach for the big Maglite flashlight I keep in bed with me, but it's rolled away onto the floor somewhere. There's nothing to do but lie here with the covers pulled up high, remembering everything.

I don't know when I go back to sleep, or if I do. I spend the rest of the night in that place between sleep and dreams and waking, my room barely illuminated by my night-light, lying in bed with my eyes open, staring at nothing at all.

Not true. Staring at the rest of my life.

How does it help to think about your entire life when it's three in the morning? What are you supposed to figure out at a time like that? And when you're sixteen like me, the rest of your life is a long, long time.

Or a very short one.

You never know. Which is just something else to think about.

"Adam!" my mother shouts.

My mother is not a dream. That much I'm sure about.

"You're going to be late for school!" she says from the foot of the stairs.

It's morning already. My mother is extremely nervous in the morning. She's super nervous at night. In between she's only relatively nervous.

"Are you awake?" she says more quietly from the other side of my door.

"For a long time," I say through the closed door.

"I had trouble sleeping, too," she says.

"Why?"

"Bad dreams," she says.

I don't respond. I wait until I hear her footsteps moving away, and then I drag myself out of bed.

I turn off my night-light and crack open the shades. The sun is harsh, tinged with yellow, hinting at the summer to come.

That's when I remember. It's the first day of tech. We move into the theater this afternoon. Our spring production opens in four days. *A Midsummer Night's Dream*.

I should be excited. I search my mind, trying to find some angle that equals excited.

"Adam!" my mother calls, now down in the kitchen. "Look at the time!"

Excited doesn't come. I'll have to settle for awake.

UP AND DOWN, UP AND DOWN.

By afternoon I've put the dream out of my head, and I'm back in my element. In the theater.

More specifically, above the theater.

I'm on a catwalk, surrounded by lighting instruments and cable, watching the actors get a tour of the set down below. I look down through layers of wire and pipe at the long line of actors snaking around the stage. The actors shouldn't be in here at all, not during load-in when we're working on lights and set, but Derek loves to break the rules almost as much as he loves to make them. Derek Dunkirk, student production designer. Man of many gifts, lover of many women, and wearer of many keys on his belt.

And my nemesis.

Maybe *nemesis* is too strong of a word. For someone to be a proper nemesis, they at least have to know you exist.

But I'm no more than an annoyance to Derek, a techie flea in his royal fur.

Derek is the first student ever invited to design a production in our high-school theater. He's doing set, lights, *and* costumes. That's not just impressive; it's legendary. Usually the director designs the show at our school. There are kids who do little things in a classroom—an improv performance or a workshop without any tech or something—but at Montclair High, the nine-hundred-seat auditorium is as close as we get to the big time. And Derek is definitely big time.

"By way of inspiration, a bit of Tennyson," Derek says with his less-than-perfect British accent. A stir passes through the actors as he clears his throat. "*'Tis better to have loved and lost / Than never to have loved at all,*" he says.

"That's so sad," Johanna says, and flits her eyelids at him.

Her actor boyfriend, Wesley, pinches her to get her attention, and she punches him on the arm. The two of them hit each other so much, I'm not sure if it's love or boxing.

"Sad but true," Derek says. He lowers his head, as if in mourning.

What would you know about it? I think.

But the female actors love it. They make that *aaaawww* sound that girls make when they see a baby or a puppy.

Even Tom, the six foot six actor with a shaved head who is playing Theseus, gets a sad look in his eye.

Derek soaks it all in.

"Ladies and gentlemen," Derek says down below, "would you be so kind as to follow me?" He walks off, clapping his hands like he's herding sheep.

I look at the female actors crossing the stage, their bare legs going from white to black as they pass between pools of light. They say theater is democratic, but it's not true. There's a pecking order here just like everywhere else in high school. The leads walk in the front of the line, followed by the bit players, followed by the extras. They're the actors without lines, sometimes even without character names.

In the front of the pack are Johanna and Miranda, who are playing Hermia and Helena, the battling heroines of *A Midsummer Night's Dream*. Next to them is Jazmin Cole, the gorgeous Latina actor who plays Titania. The three of them are the female leads of our school, the "it" actors, The Posse. Miranda is more athletic than Johanna, with short black hair and enormous boobs. From up here, her cleavage looks like a mini Grand Canyon. I know I shouldn't be looking down girls' shirts, especially girls I don't like, but cleavage is confusing like that. You can hate a girl but love her cleavage. That's how powerful it is.

The closest I've come to Miranda was during last year's

production of *Spring Awakening*. I wasn't on lights then. My job was to hold a flat backstage while she changed clothes behind it. I would stand there listening to the sound of her clothing coming off an inch away on the other side of the wall. She never said a word to me until one night in the middle of the run when she said, "I can hear you breathing on the other side of that thing, and it creeps me out."

Anyway, actors and techies don't mix at Montclair. We don't even talk to each other unless it's absolutely necessary. It's like the Hundred Years' War, only it's a hundred years of silent treatment. Nobody knows why, but it's a rule. One of about a thousand in our school. Unspoken rules. Spoken rules. Codes of conduct. Determiners of status.

I know all of these actors by name, but none of them know me. That's because I'm a guy who works behind the scenes. Some people call us stagehands, some say crew, and some say techies. Usually there's a dismissive tone in their voice when they say it. "He's just a techie." But when *we* say it, it's with pride.

I am Adam Ziegler, Techie. Capital T.

My best friend Reach calls us *Crewus technicalis*. Like we're some rare species.

But to the actors we're just techies, kids in black who hand them a prop or hold a penlight to guide them offstage. We're invisible, filling the cracks around them like grout between beautiful bathroom tiles.

There's a click on my headset.

"I think Derek's accent changed from British to Scottish," Reach says.

I free one hand, key the microphone.

"And there's some stiffness in his pantaloons," I say. "What do you think it means?"

"It means there are females in the vicinity."

"Females? I had no idea."

"Of course not. You're having a love affair with light."

"You got light, what else do you need?"

"Human beings," Reach says.

"Overrated," I say.

"Let's respect protocol on the radio," a voice says in my ear. It's our stage manager, Ignacio. You're supposed to announce yourself when you get on the headset, but Ignacio loves to creep on without anyone knowing. He's sneaky like that.

Reach says, "Are you off your meds, Ignacio?" Ignacio has ADHD, which makes it tough to have a conversation with him, but it makes him a great stage manager. I guess split focus is helpful in a job where you deal with a thousand things at once.

"I took my pill this morning!" Ignacio says. "And I expect you both to act like professionals."

"We are professionals," Reach says, "but it's a load-in, for God's sake, not the Kennedy Center Honors."

"Chain of command," Ignacio says.

That's his favorite phrase in the world. Probably because he's very near the top of the chain.

"You're right," I say. "Apologies, Ignacio. From both of us."

Reach coughs and says "suck-up" at the same time. You never cough into your mic. It's rule one of headset etiquette. Reach knows the rules better than anyone. He loves rules, but he also loves to bust Ignacio's balls.

I'm not a suck-up. I've just got plans. Things I want to do.

Shows I want to light.

I want to be a lighting designer. Too bad Derek has that job on lockdown. He's been working for two and a half years to design a big show, and our director, Mr. Apple, finally gave him the chance.

Now that he's ascended, there's not much room for me.

Derek was a legend long before I got to this school. His dad is Thomas Dunkirk, world-famous British architect, on the boards of museums and arts organizations from New York to London. Derek keeps promising his dad will come to school to do a seminar or something, but so far, nobody has ever met the guy. We've only seen him on TV.

You'd expect a kid like Derek to be at private school. I

mean, Montclair is an amazing place, but it's still a public school. Someone once asked Derek why he was here, and he said his father wanted him to be a real American boy— fit in with the plebes, so to speak—so he refused to send him away.

Lucky us.

On top of that, Derek's accent has a magical effect on women. When he speaks, they laugh at his jokes and their eyes widen. If I'd known an accent was so powerful, I might have worked on one while I was in eighth grade. I could have arrived at high school two years ago with a cool foreign identity. Instead I came in as The Guy Whose Dad Just Died. Some people could work the angles on that, get some pity love. *Postmortem poon*, as Reach calls it. But the idea makes me feel sick. Anyway, I couldn't talk to girls before Dad died; I didn't magically gain a new skill set after the funeral.

"Stay focused," Ignacio says as if he can read my mind. "Especially you, Z. Last I looked, you were twenty feet in the air."

More like twenty-five, but Ignacio's right. You don't want to be daydreaming when you're up in the air straddling a pipe.

"Will do," I say. "Z out."

I take a final glance at the girls, then I crack my knuckles and get down to business.

I shift my balance towards the pipe, pull a wrench from my belt, and lock down the C-clamp on the closest Leko. I attach a safety cable and double-check it.

It's not easy to do lights from the catwalk because I have to hang over the front in a scary way. But I've developed my own system. It saves a lot of time because I don't have to bring in a lift or keep moving a ladder around.

I finish the Leko and move down the line. Twenty-five lights down, fifteen to go.

That's the process. We load in the lights. Then we focus. Then we dry tech. Then the actors join us, and it really gets interesting.

I look across the grid at the instruments waiting to be hung. I think about the type of light each one throws. The soft fuzz of the Fresnel, the tight focus of the Leko, the bright wash of the PAR can. Then there are the gels—translucent colored sheets placed in front of the lights to change the color of the beam. I love setting up lights. Cold metal in the air is all potential, like stepping outside right before dawn when you know the world is about to change.

Reach is right about one thing: I spend a lot of time thinking about light, and it's not my job. As a techie, I don't need to think about light in general. I need to think about *a* light—the one I'm working on. I'm supposed to follow the lighting plot and mind my own business. A lighting plot is a map, shapes on a piece of paper telling me where to hang and how to focus and color each light, but when I look at the plot, it's like the lights are already turned on in my head.

As I glance at it now, it seems like Derek has made a design error. There's a dead area just left of center, a wide swath of shadow. Derek thinks there's plenty of light there because he's hanging nearly everything that exists in the school. It's his first show as a production designer, and he wants it to be the greatest debut in history. Even though the play is *A Midsummer Night's Dream*, he's designed it like a stadium rock concert—crazy set pieces, wild costumes, and a ton of metal in the air.

While it's true that there will be plenty of light onstage, in this center left area, at least, you won't be able to see the actors' faces. And it's a strange thing about light in the theater—if you can't see the actors' faces, you can't hear them very well. It's like your ears need your eyes or they get confused.

I should say something to Derek, but I won't. Derek is the reigning King of Theater, and you don't get on the king's good side by telling him how to do his job. In fact that's a good way to end up teching the actors' toilets.

Just then Derek comes back onstage with the actors in tow. Wesley struts in front of the pack, trying to stay close to Derek.

"Please mind the gap," Derek says. "I don't want any of you lovely ladies to hurt yourselves on my set."

"Be careful, ladies," Wesley says, parroting him.

There's a female actor I don't know at the very back of the pack, standing with the extras. She's not looking at Derek. She's looking up at the lights. Up towards me.

That's weird because actors rarely look up. Maybe the very first time they walk into the theater freshman year, but after that, the theater itself becomes invisible. And light? They don't care where it's coming from. They just want to make sure it's on them.

But this actor is looking everywhere, examining things. I've never seen her before, or maybe I haven't noticed her.

I notice her now.

She has long black hair and the most beautiful eyes. I can't see if they're blue or gray from here, but I think they're the kind of eyes that change color depending on the light that hits them. I get this fantasy in my head. I'm a character in a musical, a fascinating character with a troubled past. I slip down the nearest pipe and the characters freeze in place onstage, all of them except the girl with black hair. She steps out and I walk over to meet her. We don't speak right away. As the music swells, we recognize something in each other, some shared pain.

"What's your name?" she says.

"Adam Ziegler."

"Are you the director?" she says.

"Not the director," I say. "Just a techie."

Which in the musical would be a lot more noble.

Anyway, that's the fantasy.

But when she looks up again, I duck behind a pipe.

That's the reality.

Derek notices her looking around, because he says, "I have a fabulous idea. Would you like to see how the lights work?"

Derek is smooth like that. He's one of those guys who takes his shot with every girl, actors *and* techies. That's totally unheard of in my school because actors and techies don't mix here. They don't even speak unless it's to hurl insults at one another. Derek is the only one who can cross the line between the two.

"I've seen lights before," Wesley says, unimpressed.

"Not like these, you haven't," Derek says.

"I'd like to see them," Miranda says, and she smiles at Derek.

That's all the encouragement he needs.

"Your wish is my command," Derek says.

Derek signals the light board operator, Benno.

"Are you sure?" Benno says, stroking his mutton chops. Benno looks like a character from a Dickens novel, the main difference being that Dickens was obsessed with social injustice and Benno is obsessed with large boobs.

"I'm never less than sure," Derek says.

He should know you don't turn on the lights during load-in, especially not with actors in the theater. There's cable all over the place, the board hasn't been checked, and who knows what's been plugged in? But Derek doesn't care about any of that. He cares about looking good.

"Stand by for lights!" Ignacio shouts.

I take my hands away from the cable I'm plugging in.

"Lights, *go*," Ignacio says.

Benno types something into the lighting computer.

There's a loud *click*, and the theater fills with light, everything to 100 percent at the same time. Nothing is gelled, nothing is focused. There's burning white light everywhere.

For a second the theater feels like it's vibrating, light saturating every inch of the space—

Then there's a loud *snap*, and it all goes black.

TOO HIGH TO BE
ENTHRALL'D TO LOW.

The actors scream. It's more like a mock scream than a real one, but it's still kind of scary.

"Everybody freeze!" Ignacio shouts.

I stop on the catwalk, high above the theater in the darkness.

I feel panic in my chest. It's hard to breathe.

It's just a blackout, I say to myself. *No big deal. You've been through dozens of them.*

It's true. I've been through dozens, maybe even hundreds in the last two years.

But my mind starts to go places when it's dark.

Scary places.

That's why I always keep extra light on me. I have a glow stick in my right front pocket, a penlight in my left, a mini Mag on my belt. That's just for starters. All I have to do is grab one and take it out.

But I can't move. The dark feels vast and empty, like standing on the edge of a canyon.

I try to slow my breathing and calm myself down, but it's not working.

The dream.

I'm back in the dream from last night, my father stepping out of the gloom to stand near me. I don't think the dream ever goes away. It just advances and retreats inside my head, ducking out of sight long enough for me to forget about it, then popping up to reassert itself.

My father is next to me now, but there's no way to keep him there. He'll be gone again any moment, lost in darkness.

"That's a Rothko," Dad says.

I'm eight years old standing in front of a painting at the MoMA in New York. Dad and I used to go there a lot. We took the train from Montclair into the city every Sunday. Dad would choose a museum for us, and we'd spend hours looking at art. Then we'd walk through Central Park together, talking about what we'd seen.

I'm back there with him now, standing in front of this burst of orange red on the wall.

"What do you think?" Dad says.

I look at it for a few seconds, but I don't see much, only bands of color.

"It's okay," I say.

Dad says, "Give it a chance."

He puts his hand on my shoulder, willing me to stay.

I look at the painting. I look at my dad.

"Wait," he whispers.

I wait.

The painting starts to move, the canvas vibrating with color.

"Now what do you see?" Dad says.

"It's alive," I say.

"Where are the damn lights?!" Derek shouts.

The museum evaporates. I'm back in the theater, standing high in the air.

My father is gone.

I can still smell him, feel the warmth where his hand touched my shoulder.

The house lights come back on. Black stage in front, empty theater seats below. The actors are clustered onstage, some of the girls with their arms around one another.

"What happened to the lights?" Johanna says.

Derek's face turns purple. "Son of a bitch!" he says. He looks around the theater until his eyes settle on Ignacio.

Ignacio gulps hard. He looks around the theater until he finds Benno.

Benno shrugs. "I think the dimmers blew," he says. "Maybe something was plugged in wrong?"

He looks around for someone else to blame. People

are ducking out of sight, slumping down behind seat backs, sliding offstage.

I don't slump or slide. I stand there, still thinking about Rothko and my father.

Benno, Ignacio, and Derek all look up at the same time.

I can imagine what it looks like. Me standing with a cable in my hand. Guilty as hell.

"That kid up there. I always forget his name," Derek says.

"Adam Ziegler," Ignacio says. "Z."

He doesn't even pause before he says it, like maybe he's considering covering for me. He just gives me up.

I'm watching this happen, but it seems far away, like it's got very little to do with me. A lot of my life seems like that now.

Derek's face curls into a snarl.

"Get your butt down here, Ziegler!"

"I didn't do anything," I say.

"Z!" Derek screams. He taps his foot.

I cross the catwalk, the creaking metal loud in the theater below.

"What's going on out there?" Reach says in my headset.

"Firing squad," I say.

I walk to the edge of the catwalk where a ladder leads to the stage floor below.

I glance down. The Posse looks up at me, the girls

putting their hands on their hips in unison like a cheer-leader move.

Everyone is looking at me. Sweat breaks out on my forehead. The floor seems like it's a thousand miles away.

"I'm coming for you," Reach says in my ear, and I hear a scraping sound as he rips off the headset.

I take two steps down the ladder, and I stop. My mind is reeling.

The girl with long black hair is onstage looking up at me, or at least at my ass sticking out from the ladder. Not what I'd call a great first impression.

"What the hell is wrong with that kid?" Derek says.

Good question.

I want to climb down and tell them I had nothing to do with it, but I can't.

I'm stuck on the ladder, high in the air, caught between up and down.

I hear footsteps running onstage.

"Rishekesh Patel at your service," Reach says to Derek.

Reach to the rescue.

"How can I help?" Reach says.

"You can get this jerk down," Derek says.

"What did this jerk do now?" Reach says.

The girls laugh a little.

"He blew up my lights," Derek says. "What if Mr. Apple were here? What would he think?"

He would think you screwed up, I say to myself. Mr. Apple weighs five hundred pounds, and four hundred ninety-nine of them are vicious. He doesn't like people making mistakes on his stage. He's fine if you make a legitimate mistake, because that's how you learn. But not a *stupid* mistake. A stupid mistake earns you a face full of sour Apple.

"The last thing I need is a techie screwing up my design," Derek says.

The way he says *techie* makes me wince.

I look up towards the catwalk. *Climb*, my head says. *Get away*.

The stage lights come back on. Not at full, but at 25 percent. Benno is testing the board.

"Looks like we got the lights back for you, Double D," Reach says.

Derek scowls. He hates that name.

Reach smiles like he has absolutely no idea he did anything wrong.

I have to give it to Reach. He has the ability to make fun of Derek and kiss ass at the same time. That's a major skill set.

"What are we going to do about ladder boy?" Derek says.

"A public thrashing," Reach says. "I suggest you whip him with a cable. Twenty lashes."

The girls laugh even more. Derek looks at them, trying to figure out if he's being made fun of. After a second, he smiles.

"We shall make him walk the plank," Derek says, his accent turning him into the ship captain from *The Pirates of Penzance*. "Or perhaps he needs to be removed from the crew?"

Does Derek have the right to fire me? Not exactly. But he could get me fired. A few words to Mr. Apple and I would be out the door.

I think about a life without techies. Without theater. Without light.

"What if we have him gas up your car?" Reach says.

Derek's car is his pride and joy, a bright red BMW convertible that he loves more than life itself.

"That's a fine idea," Derek says, now smiling.

He walks offstage with the actors following behind.

The girl with black hair hangs back for a second. She stares up at me. There's a look in her eyes, a familiar look. It's the kind of look I got all the time after Dad died.

She pities me.

I start to climb as fast as I can, scurrying up the ladder until I'm back on the catwalk where I can breathe.

THAT WAY GOES
THE GAME.

Two minutes later Reach's head pops over the side of the rail.

"That was a close call," he says.

"Thanks for bailing me out."

"Where there is a sinking boat, there will always be Rishekesh."

It pisses me off that Reach is always trying to save me. The worst part is that I kind of need saving.

"So what happened up there?" Reach says.

"I froze."

"Because of Derek? He's all sound and fury."

"Not Derek. The blackout."

"That again," Reach says.

He takes a long breath, gives me the *I'm worried about you* look. My mother has the same look. I hate that look.

When we were ten, Reach and I made a pact that we would tell each other everything. There would be no secrets between us. It's one of those agreements kids make all the time and then forget about six months later.

Only we never forgot.

So Reach knows me really well. He knows about the dream, about what happens to me in the dark.

"I thought it was getting better," he says.

"I thought so, too," I say.

It's getting worse. But I don't say that. I don't want to worry him.

Reach thinks about it for a second, one thick eyebrow raised high on his forehead.

"It's no big deal," he says. "You're under a lot of pressure. A show going into tech, Derek breathing down your hole—"

"What if I freak out during a show?" I say.

"You won't."

"But what if I do?"

"It's just fear," Reach says. "We all have fears."

"Except you."

"Not true. I have fears."

"Like what?"

"Like shrinkage. And my mother."

Reach's mom is a total control freak. Their house is like a supermax prison, only the food is spicier.

"I'll keep an eye on you," Reach says. "And if you need anything . . ."

Reach wiggles his cell phone in my direction.

"I'll call," I say.

"Promise?" he says.

"Promise."

But what am I going to do? Call Reach in the middle of the night and tell him I'm having a bad dream?

"I can't afford to lose you," Reach says. "Who would tell me his problems?"

"Half Crack has lots of problems."

Half Crack is a crew guy who never wears a belt. When he bends over, the room clears out.

"He's got little boy problems," Reach says. "I need man issues. Hard-core crises. Something I can sink my teeth into."

I look away, busying myself with a lamp change.

"What was the deal with the blackout?" Reach says.

"Derek has too much stuff in the air. He's maxing out the dimmer packs."

"Why don't you tell him?"

"I did tell him. He said to make it work, so I'm making it work."

"Go over his head," Reach says.

"I like my job, limited and lowly though it may be."

I know better than to get between Derek and his

ambitions. Tech crew is paved with the bodies of techies who tried it.

"You should be designing this show," Reach says.

"Let's not go there," I say.

I glance down, making sure nobody's below to overhear us.

Reach says, "If it weren't for his father, Derek would still be backstage coiling cable with the rest of us."

"His father didn't get him the production designer position," I say.

"Yeah, but it sure didn't hurt. Think about it from Mr. Apple's perspective. You give a kid with a famous father a big job, then the father comes to see the show, you buddy up to him a little—"

"And what? You get a job at his architecture firm?"

"No, you ask him to introduce you to some of his famous theater friends. Or you make him a patron. Or whatever. You don't know much about kissing ass, do you?"

"I know nothing."

Reach gets this look on his face, the one he gets when he's brewing up a plan.

"I'd love to take Derek down a couple notches," he says softly. "What would happen if we stopped covering his ass?"

"He'd burn down the theater."

"Is that so bad?"

"It depends how many people are in it."

"What if it were freshmen?" Reach says. "Or better yet, freshman *actors*."

"That's terrible," I say, but I laugh a little. Reach hates actors even more than he hates freshmen. And he hates his mother more than either of them.

"I sense an evil plan coming together," I say.

"It could be *our* evil plan. Like the old days," Reach says.

Reach and I used to think up all kinds of plots when we were kids. Once we stole three tubes of paint from my dad and painted Reach's dog. Actually, it was Reach's *mom's* dog. Reach was grounded for three months after that, and he had to go to Hindi school on the weekends.

"Remember when we painted my mom's dog?" Reach says.

I laugh. "I was just thinking about that."

"So what do you say we take on the Big Bad Brit together?"

I wish I could talk to my brother Josh right now. This is the kind of thing he knows all about—when to push forward and when to retreat. But he's at Cornell and impossible to get ahold of.

Reach is still looking at me, waiting for an answer.

"I'll try repatching some of the circuits, distribute the

load," I say. "It might hold if Derek doesn't keep adding things."

"So that's a *no* from you," he says.

"It's a no."

"How do we turn it into a *yes*?"

"I don't want to have this conversation again," I say. Because we've had this conversation a thousand times. Reach tries to get me to hang out with the guys; I say no. Reach plans for us to meet girls at some techie party in Paramus; I say no. Reach comes up with a crazy plan and I say no.

Reach throws up his hands like he's surrendering.

But he never surrenders. Not really.

COME, TEARS, CONFOUND.

There's one bad thing about being up on the catwalk for a long time: no bathroom facilities. After five hours, my bladder feels like the pressure hull of a nuclear sub. I've heard that some professional lighting guys keep a soda bottle on the catwalk for emergencies. That's hard-core tech, too hard-core even for me. I already have a negative rep. I don't need to be the kid on the ceiling with a collection of piss bottles.

I'm still feeling embarrassed about the ladder incident, so I keep looking over the side, waiting for the actors to go away. When the theater clears, it takes me like five seconds to get down. It figures. With nobody around, I'm like a mountain goat.

I'm rushing offstage when I hear a strange whimpering sound from the wings. It sounds like Mr. Apple brought his dog to school again, even though it's against the rules. He has a little Lhasa Apso named Carol Channing. It's quite a sight to see a five-hundred-pound man with a two-pound dog. But Carol is his pride and joy. Mr. Apple is known to go on a rampage when she gets lost. If she's loose in the theater, I'd better find her.

"Carol Channing," I call as I walk towards the wings.

No answer. Just more whimpering.

"Hello, Dolly?" I say.

I turn the corner, and I see two feet peeking out from behind a flat.

"Go away," a girl's voice says.

I stick my head around the corner. It's Grace Navarro, a girl who joined the tech crew a couple months ago. She's crying and sniffling. She uses the back of her hand to wipe snot from her nose.

Gross.

"What's wrong with me?" she says.

"I don't know," I say.

"That was a rhetorical question," Grace says, kind of nasty.

"Whatever," I say, and I start to walk away.

"I'm sorry. I'm not angry at you. I'm angry at myself," Grace says.

I look back at her, tears running down her almond cheeks. I can't stand it when a girl cries.

I reach into my tech pack and come up with a tissue. I hand it to Grace.

"He said I was his favorite," she says, blowing her nose hard. "And I believed him. How stupid."

That's when I remember: Grace was going out with Derek a little while ago. Maybe "going out" is not the right expression. Derek burns through new girls so quickly, we stopped learning their names and started calling them DNF. Derek's New Frosh.

So Grace was DNF. Temporarily.

I'm already on Derek's shit list, but if anyone sees me talking to this girl, I might cross over the line onto his dead-meat list.

I should walk away and leave her to her meltdown. But then I think about my mother crying in the bathroom after dad died. She never wanted me to see her, so she'd hide in there and close the door, thinking I wouldn't hear the whimpering noises. But I heard everything.

"My heart is broken," Grace says.

Now I can't leave her alone.

"Come with me," I say, and I pull her into the Cave.

WHERE THE BOLT OF CUPID FELL.

The Cave is our electrics room and the unofficial home of the techies. Usually the place is packed with lighting instruments, but Derek has nearly everything onstage or up on the catwalk waiting to be hung. There are a couple broken instruments scattered on the floor and a single lightbulb overhead.

"Here's what kills me," Grace says. "He acts like it never happened. But I still have the mark."

She tilts her head back and points to a black-and-blue circle the size of a nickel under her chin. A hickey under the chin. The Mark of Derek. Nobody can figure out how he gets under there. Reach says he has an extendable jaw like the Alien.

"It's fading," she says, "but it's still there. You can see it, right?"

"A little," I say.

"More than a little," Grace says. "It's the Scarlet Letter. That's why nobody will talk to me."

"It's more than that," I say. "It's because you broke the rule."

If a girl ends up with Derek, she gets exiled from the techies. I'm not talking about a little silent treatment. I'm talking serious, Techie-in-the-Iron-Mask stuff. It's kind of ironic. I mean, high school is all about who's in and who's out, and by almost any measure, techies are out. You don't get onto the crew riding a wave of popularity, so you'd think we'd have this open, compassionate system, but we don't. The only difference between techies and everyone else is that you don't get rejected by us because you look funny or have dyslexia or zits or something. Those are more or less prerequisites.

For techies it's about two things: skill set and loyalty.

If you have one, you make the crew.

If you have both, you stay forever.

But there are a few things you don't do. Certain rules that demand banishment:

You don't rat people out.

You don't betray another techie.

You don't get friendly with actors. You don't talk to them at all, unless you're telling them where to stand or how not to electrocute themselves.

And if you're a girl and you want to be on the crew, you don't date Derek.

Simple, right?

"What was I thinking?" she says.

"Good question."

"Maybe . . . I thought I was in love."

"People do crazy things when they're in love," I say.

"Have you ever been in love?" she says.

"No."

She looks away like maybe I shouldn't be commenting on something I know nothing about. I can't really disagree with her.

"But I know what it's like to miss someone," I say.

"Yeah?" she says.

Her face softens. The lightbulb is swinging slightly in the air above us. I hear the sound of hammering onstage, a distant *tap tap* that echoes through the Cave. I think about what we look like sitting here together, two bodies in a pool of light.

"So you do get it," Grace says.

"A little. Yeah."

"You want to know the craziest thing of all?" she says. "I want him back."

I think about Dad.

"That's not so crazy," I say.

She smiles.

"You're a good guy, Z."

"That's what my mom tells me," I say.

Grace laughs and looks around the Cave. On the far side is the Techie Wall of Fame, where we hang the pictures of people when they get accepted into the Light and Set Club. All of our pictures are there, posed with these crazy Elvis glasses Reach bought at a street fair in Hoboken. That's how you know you've made it as a techie. You get a space on the wall where you can pose like a bad Elvis impersonator.

"I still want to be a techie," she says. "I've got serious skill set."

"What do you do?"

"I can fix anything. I've been working on our house since I was twelve. My father picks up a hammer and his IQ drops to single digits."

"It sounds like you'd make a good set carpenter."

An idea pops into my head. A way to get Grace on the crew permanently.

"I think I've got a plan," I say.

"What kind of plan?"

Her face gets this hopeful look, the same kind of look Reach got last year when a cute exchange student appeared in school and didn't know she was supposed to avoid techies.

"Lay low for a while," I say. "I'll put in a word for you

35

with the guys. Then we wait for them to come around."

Her face gets this disappointed look, the same one Reach got when the cute exchange student realized techies were social anthrax.

"It's not much of a plan," she says.

"I know."

It's just not the same coming up with a plan without Reach. The evil genius aspect is missing.

"I'll refine the plan as we go along," I say.

"You think it will work?" she says.

I try to remember a time someone has made it back from techie exile, but I can't.

"Just don't quit," I say. "Whatever you do."

Because that's the last of the techie rules:

You don't quit, no matter how hard things get.

I MAY HIDE MY FACE.

I promise Grace I'll put in a good word for her, and I rush off to the bathroom. I pee for what seems like ten hours. Someone has scratched LOZER on the wall over the urinal. I'm not sure if they were aiming for *loser* and misspelled it, or there's some kid named Lozer who wants the world to know his name. Either way, it's depressing.

I finish my business, then I turn on the water to wash my hands.

The light flickers over my head along with the familiar buzzing of a fluorescent bulb going bad. It's like a scene from *Little Shop of Horrors*.

I study my reflection in the mirror.

Adam Ziegler. Skinny guy. Angry acne.

I don't get regular acne. My acne rises up from the depths like a volcano. I would kill to have normal zits, zits you can pop, nice clean whiteheads that beg to be pinched. Instead I get these rock-hard swellings that make me look like a freak. I'm always turning to one side or the other to hide them. Which side is the least broken out that day? That's the side I present to the world.

Today I've got zero options. Both sides are terrible. I've got two zits like twin moons orbiting my nose.

I take a tube of greasepaint out of my pocket. Every once in a while I borrow makeup from the actors' dressing room for an emergency cover-up. I use a dab now to hide the damage.

The light buzzes again. The horror-movie flicker distorting my face in the mirror.

That's when I hear it. Heavy breathing.

At first I think it's my imagination. Part of the horror soundtrack in my head.

"Hello?" I say.

The breathing stops.

A second later it starts again, even louder. It's not my imagination. There's panting and something else. A crinkling sound.

It's coming from one of the stalls.

"Is someone here?" I say.

The panting gets louder. Are people having sex in here?

I should take off and leave them to it, but what if it's not sex? What if someone needs help?

I look down the row of stalls. They're all completely open except the last one. The door is shut, but not all the way.

There's a custodian's mop leaning against the wall. I pick it up and use the long stick to push the door open . . .

"Holy crap!" I say.

It's Mr. Apple.

He's sitting on the toilet fully dressed, his massive body filling the tiny stall. He holds a brown paper bag over his mouth and breathes heavily, the bag shrinking and expanding with each breath.

"Should I get the nurse?" I say.

Mr. Apple holds up a finger. *Wait a minute.*

"Panic—" he says.

He takes a deep breath, nearly inhaling the bag into his lungs.

"—attack," he says.

He breathes out. The bag expands.

"Panic attack?" I say.

He nods.

I know what it's like to panic. I've never had to breathe into a bag, but I've freaked out a lot of times. In the dark. On the ladder. And those are just the most recent.

Two more slow breaths, and Mr. Apple puts the bag down and leans back. The walls of the stall rattle.

"Who are you?" Mr. Apple says.

"Adam Ziegler. I'm on the crew."

"I thought I'd seen you before."

"Can I get you anything? Water?"

"How about morphine?"

"We used it all at the last cast party."

Mr. Apple smiles.

"A techie with a sense of humor. That's a nice treat. Be a good fellow and bring me some wet paper towels."

I hurry over to the sink and hold a wad of towels under the water.

"Are you sick?" I say.

"Sick of my life," Mr. Apple calls out from the stall.

And then the heavy breathing starts again.

I rush back with the paper towels. Mr. Apple takes the towels and presses them to his face.

"Let me ask you a question, Mr. Ziegler. Is it as bad as it looks?"

"This bathroom?"

"My show."

Is the show bad? I hadn't really thought about it. I've been so busy trying to get the lights right, I never really thought about the production as a whole

Still, Mr. Apple looks so pitiful, I have to say something.

"It's not so bad," I say. "I mean, it's getting better."

"A tiny bit of advice—don't become an actor."

"Why not?"

"You're a terrible liar. But thank you for trying."

Mr. Apple blinks hard several times and grabs for the bag. The panting starts again, the brown paper expanding and contracting.

"Is it okay if I go back to the theater?" I say.

He nods for me to go.

"This," he says, gesturing to himself in the stall, "is our secret."

"I promise," I say.

"Good lad," he says, and he waves me away with a free hand.

SPIRITS OF
ANOTHER SORT.

I come out of the bathroom into the long empty hall. I'm thinking about what Mr. Apple said about the show.

Is it really bad?

That's the thing about the theater. Everyone tends to worry about themselves, whether they look good. Actors want to act, techies want to tech.

Who's thinking about the big picture?

The director. Mr. Apple.

No wonder he needs a paper bag.

I stop in the hall and lean against the cool surface of the wall. I see the way the light bounces off the gloss paint, some of it reflected upward, some absorbed into the linoleum on the floor.

"Stand here, Adam," Dad said one summer afternoon in his painting studio. He gestured to a place across the room, at an angle to the window. "Look at the light."

I looked and saw a bright, sunlit room.

"Now watch," Dad said, and he picked up a pile of chalk shavings from his workbench. He stepped over to the light, held up his palm, and blew hard.

The shavings flew into the stream of light, and what seemed like bright sunshine in general became a dozen shafts of light, each a river of light moving through space on its own trajectory.

"You can't see light itself," Dad said. "You only see light's reflection."

I look down the hallway now, at all the places light is reflected.

A fairy comes walking around the corner at the far end of the hallway. She's in bare feet with white flowing gauze around her, long black hair falling in clumps at her shoulders. When she steps into the light, the sparkles in the gauze twinkle like stars.

It's the dark-haired actress from the theater, the one who looked up while everyone was looking down. She stops in the light, and I shrink back into the shadows and watch her.

"Hail, mortal!" she says.

At first I think she's speaking to me, but then she looks in the opposite direction, raises her hand in greeting, and says again, *"Hail, mortal."*

It's Peaseblossom's line. Peaseblossom is one of the

fairy characters in the play. She has maybe three or four lines and a couple scenes. Nothing much.

The girl takes a shuffling sideways step and starts to spin. The fabric in her costume swirls around, and the skirt starts to rise. I look at her bare legs. They're very pale, white and pink and speckled in that way pale people are so you can see the veins beneath their skin. She keeps dancing, and the skirt keeps rising. It goes higher and higher until I see a flash of bright red underwear.

A girl's underwear is such a private thing. If you know what color it is, it's like knowing this huge secret. You can never look at her the same way again. Every time you see her, you can only think about her underwear.

Now I know three people's secrets. Grace's, Mr. Apple's, and the fairy's. That's a lot of secrets for one day.

The fairy girl spins one more time, then she starts to practice a dance move from the play. She points her toe and steps forward with one leg, trying to do a kind of curtsy, but she screws it up midway, tripping over herself.

She curses and punches herself in the thigh. This is a violent fairy. She tries the move again, a look of deep concentration on her face. This time she does the curtsy, then stops, noticing me for the first time.

Her mouth puckers and she lets out a surprised, "Oh."

She tugs at her skirt.

"I didn't know anyone was there," she says.

I try to speak, but nothing comes out.

She says, "I'm not going to see that on YouTube, am I? Fairies Gone Wild."

I want to laugh, but my mouth isn't working right.

"Okay, you're creeping me out just the tiniest bit," she says.

I want to tell her that I'm the lighting guy, she doesn't have to be afraid.

I want to tell her my name.

I want to tell her how pretty she is.

But it all sounds stupid in my head. I'm a zit-faced techie with a dead father, standing in the dark looking at her legs. That's not exactly high romance.

A moment passes, the two of us watching each other.

"Okay, I'm going to head back to the Fairy Factory now," she says, backing away down the hall.

I have to say something to her. . . .

But I don't.

I watch her go, her pale legs receding farther and farther until they disappear in shadow at the end of the hall.

SORROW'S HEAVINESS DOTH HEAVIER GROW.

I'm a coward. There's no other word for it.

I'm on the catwalk trying to hang and focus the rest of the lights, but I keep thinking about it. I don't understand how I can run around twenty-five feet in the air and handle dangerous electrics, but when it comes to girls, I'm Chicken Little.

The idea makes my zits ache.

I move from light to light, trying to lose myself in work. I push the actress out of my head. It's important not to get distracted when you're teching. That's how people get hurt.

At some point Ignacio walks onstage pulling the ghost light with him. The ghost light is a bare lightbulb on a pole that burns downstage center when nobody is in the theater. It's one of those theater superstitions, like not saying the name of a certain Scottish play or telling people to "break a leg" instead of "good luck." Some people say we need a ghost light because ghosts roam the theater at night, and they'll get angry if they can't see where they're going. Other people say the light is like a talisman that keeps ghosts away from the theater in the first place. Reach has a more practical explanation. He says the ghost light is there so the last person out of the theater and the first person in don't trip and kill themselves in the dark.

"You almost done?" Ignacio says.

"Can I get five more minutes?" I say.

"I'm out of here, but Mr. Apple is still around."

No kidding. He's probably breathing into a paper bag in his office right now.

I wave to Ignacio. He plugs in the light and exits.

I look at the glow of the ghost light on the empty stage. There's something sad about it, like the last streetlight in a deserted town.

I lean back and lay my head on a sweatshirt on the catwalk. I'm not planning to go to sleep, only rest for a minute. I've barely put my head down before I'm back in the school hallway in my dreams, looking at the pools of light and shadow that hopscotch the long hall.

"I used to love you," a girl says. It's the actress with long black hair, the one playing Peaseblossom. She dances down the hall, spinning until I see her red panties.

I know it's crazy that a girl I've never met is talking

about being in love with me. But it's one of those dream things—it's true in the dream even if it's a lie in real life.

"You don't love me anymore?" I say.

"Not anymore."

"What can I do?"

"Nothing to do, nothing to be done," the fairy girl says. *"You can't change the past."*

I don't even get to have a girlfriend in a dream. I only get to have a breakup. Sad.

The surprising thing is how much it hurts when she says it. There's this deep ache in my chest, like the time I had bronchitis for two weeks and I could feel my lungs hurting.

"It's a shame," she says.

But her voice sounds different now, like a man's voice.

"I used to love this," a man says.

I open my eyes.

I'm up on the catwalk. My head has slipped off the sweatshirt, and it's resting on cold metal. I glance down to the floor where Mr. Apple is lying on a chaise longue in the middle of the stage, his enormous bulk draped over the sides, a cell phone pressed to his ear.

He says, "I used to love the theater, Sylvester. Now I hate it."

He dangles one foot to the floor where Carol Channing lies next to him. He slips off his loafer and rubs her fur a little too hard with his pudgy toes. She yelps and scurries away from him.

"Don't tell me it's not that bad," Mr. Apple says. "You should have seen the last rehearsal. Shakespeare turned over in his grave, threw up, then rolled into his own vomit. And whose fault is that? Mine! I'm the atrocious director of an atrocious production. This is what it's come to, Syl. I'm not only a high-school drama teacher, I'm a *terrible* high-school drama teacher."

It feels bad to listen in on Mr. Apple's private call, but I'm stuck. If I say something now, he'll know I've heard the whole conversation.

"I'm doing everything I can," Mr. Apple says, "but I have no inspiration, sweetie. It's like the lights are off. It's Midsummer in the dark."

He scratches at one of his stomach folds.

"Of course *you* inspire me, Sylvester, but in a different way. My God, why do you have to take everything so personally?"

I shift on the catwalk and my arm hits a gel frame.

Mr. Apple stops in mid-sentence.

"Hello?" he says.

He pauses for a moment, then says into the phone:

"I've got to go, honey. I'll be home in a little bit. Dinner sounds nice. You know I love your salmon croquettes."

He hangs up.

"I hate salmon croquettes," he says to no one in particular.

He hefts himself up to a sitting position on the chaise.

"Is someone here?" he says.

He looks around the theater, scanning everywhere. Then he looks up in my direction. Does he see me? I can't be sure.

Derek rushes in.

"I've got it!" he says.

"They have medicine that will get rid of it," Mr. Apple says.

Silence.

"That was a joke," Mr. Apple says.

"Yes, sir. Very funny," Derek says.

Mr. Apple sighs, unappreciated. "All right, Mr. Dunkirk, what do you have for me?"

"An amazing inspiration," Derek says.

"I can't wait to hear it. But why don't you start by telling me what inspired the blackout earlier?"

"You heard about that?" Derek says.

"I'm the director. An actor passes gas in the dressing room and I get a memo. Often a long memo."

Derek shuffles from foot to foot. I don't think I've ever seen him nervous before.

"That blackout was a fluke," Derek says.

"A fluke is a onetime event. We've had set problems,

light problems, even costume problems. That's not a fluke. It's a trend."

"This one was not my fault. One of the techies made an error."

"Which one?" Mr. Apple says.

"The lighting guy, Adam Ziegler. You know him?"

"I do," Mr. Apple says.

I flash on Mr. Apple in the bathroom stall, mopping his forehead with wet towels.

"I'll get rid of him," Derek says.

Mr. Apple scratches at his goatee, thinking.

I have to speak up now. I have to defend myself.

But how I can explain a blackout when I don't know why it happened?

"Here's what I think . . . ," Mr. Apple says.

I try to say something, but I can't.

This is how it ends. I'm going to sit up here and watch myself getting thrown off the crew, and I'm going to do nothing. Because that's what a coward does.

"I understand that you're a student and there's a lot of pressure on you," Mr. Apple says.

"I can handle it," Derek says quickly.

"I hope so," Mr. Apple says. "But I don't want you firing people quite yet. You're in a position of authority now. You need to take care of your people. Teach them. Guide them."

"I'd rather get rid of him," Derek says.

"You're not hearing me," Mr. Apple says. "I gave you a big opportunity on this show."

"I know you did. And I'm grateful."

"What has been given can be taken away," Mr. Apple says.

Derek's face goes pale. I can see it white and clammy on the edge of the ghost light.

"I assure you, Mr. Apple—"

Mr. Apple holds up a hand. *Silence.*

Derek takes a moment to regroup.

"This brings me to the inspiration I mentioned," he says.

"Let's hear it," Mr. Apple says, exhaustion creeping into his voice.

"I've noticed the show is lacking a certain—"

"Talent base," Mr. Apple says.

"Panache," Derek says.

"Very politic," Mr. Apple says.

"I have something I think will improve it. A spotlight."

"More light? You're going to brown out Northern Jersey."

"Not just more light," Derek says. "The perfect light."

"We can't afford any more equipment in our budget."

Mr. Apple rises from the chaise, slipping his bag over his shoulder.

"Money is no problem," Derek says. "My father will take care of it."

"I see," Mr. Apple says. "Fine, then."

He nods and walks slowly from the stage.

Derek calls after him, "About that techie—"

"No firing," Mr. Apple says.

"At least not yet," Derek says.

"That's right," Mr. Apple says. "Give the poor boy another chance."

SHE, SWEET LADY, DOTES, DEVOUTLY DOTES.

I'm walking home feeling so angry I can't see straight. I want to kill Derek for trying to get rid of me, wipe his name off the tech board, off the call sheets, off the play program forever. I think about Reach's offer to come up with a plot to bring him down. Why shouldn't I take him up on it? Derek doesn't give a crap about the work I've done for him. And if I make a mistake, I'm gone. So what do I care if Derek goes down in flames? It might even be better for me.

I don't wait for the light to change at the crosswalk, I just step into the road. A big SUV blares its horn at me. I jump back onto the sidewalk, my heart racing.

It wasn't close. But it was close enough.

The SUV guy gives me an angry fist wave, throws the truck into gear, and roars away down the street.

I'm tired of being that guy, the one who is afraid all the time. I fantasize about being brave, but I do nothing.

The fairy girl, Reach, Derek.

My whole life is like that. I need to speak my mind and I don't. I need to stick up for myself and I don't.

That's what fear does to you.

I think about the kind of person I'd be without fear. I try to imagine myself brave and honest, but I can't.

Instead I think of my brother, Josh.

He's that kind of guy; nothing fazes him.

When Josh went to school in Montclair, he pretty much ran the place. He played sports, he had clear skin, he was captain of things, and he had girlfriends. Emphasis on the plural. There were girls around Josh from as far back as I can remember. When he was in fifth grade, girls started coming over to the house to ask for him. There would be a knock at the door, and I'd open it to find some girl standing there looking nervous, biting a fingernail or twirling a strand of hair. When I asked Josh about them, he said, "They're friends. No big deal." That just confused me more, because my friends didn't show up unannounced and they didn't bring gifts.

Josh got his first actual girlfriend in seventh grade, then another more serious one in eighth. He had three or four in high school. Maybe more. I lost count. The longest was Meredith, who he dated for two years. She was gorgeous. Sometimes she came over the house when Mom wasn't home, and she and Josh would go into the den and close the door. I used to pretend it was me in the den with her instead of Josh. I'd sit in my room alone watching TV, but in my mind I was in the den with Meredith, and Josh had never been born.

I thought girls would come to the house looking for me just like they did for him. When it didn't happen in fifth, I told myself to be patient. Maybe I was a late bloomer. Then it didn't happen in sixth or seventh.

By eighth grade, I knew I was in trouble. Girls weren't going to show up for me.

Josh and I may have been brothers, but things were different for me. Girls didn't see me the same way.

I was going to have to do something, or high school was going to be terrible.

When Dad died in the summer before ninth, that was it for me. I started high school with this weight on my chest. I couldn't talk to anyone, especially girls. I could barely get up in the morning and drag myself to school. I didn't shower, didn't change my clothes. For a while everyone was super nice, but eventually people started to avoid me.

Except the techies.

Showering is kind of optional with us.

Reach brought me into the fold, and I've been there ever since, my picture up on the Techie Wall of Fame inside the Cave.

What if Josh was in the same situation as me now?

He'd know what to do.

I need to talk to Josh.

The thought hits me hard.

It's been a million years since we've spoken, and that's not right. He's my big brother, and brothers talk about things. At least they're supposed to.

So I take out my phone.

I hate dialing Josh's number. I'm sure I'm bothering him and he's going to be angry with me. Isn't that crazy, when you won't call your own brother because he might be angry?

To hell with it. I dial the number.

It rings once, twice, and then I hear Josh's voice, happy and excited.

"Hey, what's up?"

I chuckle to myself, thinking I was stupid to worry. Josh checked his caller ID, saw his baby brother, and snapped up the phone. He's even excited to hear from me. What was I so worried about?

"Hey, Josh. What's going on?" I say.

"It's Josh," his voice says. "Go ahead and leave a message. If you can make me laugh, I'll call you back."

It's one of those phone message that tricks you into thinking it's a conversation.

The phone beeps, and I hang up without saying anything. My face burns red, and I feel like an idiot all over again.

SUMMER STILL DOTH TEND UPON MY STATE.

"Are you hungry?" Mom says when I walk in the door. She's always trying to feed me because she thinks I'm too thin.

"No."

"But you've been gone all day."

"I had a granola bar at rehearsal."

"That's not enough," she says.

"I'm starving my zits. If I withhold nutrition, what choice do they have but to go elsewhere?"

"They'll stay, and you'll get too thin."

Mom opens the freezer and pokes around. Then she closes the freezer and opens the cabinet. Then she closes the cabinet and opens a drawer.

"Aha! Found them!" Mom says, and pulls a package of Milano cookies out of the drawer.

"Can I ask you a question?" I say.

"Anything," Mom says.

"It's about girls."

Mom stops what she's doing.

"Girls or girl?" she says. She seems excited, which makes me feel kind of sick inside. Mom is desperate for me to be happy. I guess that's what a mother is supposed to want, but it feels like a lot of pressure.

"It's about girls plural," I say. "At least for now."

"Okay." Mom sits across from me, biting at a fingernail.

"What do girls want?" I say.

"The same thing as you," Mom says. "What do you want?"

"Girls."

"Okay, maybe not exactly the same thing."

Mom opens the package of Milanos, sniffs at the inside, then closes them again. I notice she's looking thin, too. Not just thin, but tired.

"Do you think girls are so different?" Mom says.

"They are," I say.

"Am I?"

"You're not a girl."

"Thank you very much."

"I mean you *were* a girl, but you're a woman now."

"I still remember being a girl," Mom says, "even if it was ten thousand years ago."

"Okay," I say. "What did you want ten thousand years ago?"

Mom thinks for a second.

"Boys," she says with a laugh.

I consider that. Girls want boys as much as boys want girls. I think of Maria dancing around the stage in *West Side Story*, thrilled because she met a boy. For a second it seems like an exciting idea, but I don't believe it. Because girls don't want boys in general; they want certain boys. Boys with accents. Boys who play sports. Boys who are popular.

I don't think Mom is lying, I just don't think she has the whole story. Mom hasn't dated anyone in the two years since Dad died. And if you count her time with Dad, it's been over twenty years since she was on a date. So I can't trust her memory on things like this.

Mom sighs, looks out the kitchen window.

"Can you believe it's still light out?" she says. "And it's past seven."

She gives up on the Milanos and puts them back in the drawer.

"Have you thought about summer vacation?" she says.

"No," I say, even though I've been thinking about it a lot.

"I was thinking we could go away somewhere. You know, get away from things."

"All of us?" I say.

Mom hesitates. "Josh is doing a summer school program. So it's just you and me, kiddo."

"Big surprise," I say.

"That's not fair," Mom says. "Josh is in college now. He's got different priorities."

"Fine with me," I say, because I don't want to get into it. "You and I should do something."

"Good," Mom says.

Summertime.

We never had to think about summer before. Summer was simple. It was about painting.

Every summer Mom would take some time off from work, and we'd all go to New Hampshire, to this place outside of Concord where we had a little cabin and Dad had a painting studio down the road.

Mom, Josh, and I would leave Dad alone all day, go off to the lake or out for a hike. We'd come back together at the end of the day. Dad would put something on the grill and we'd spend the night as a family, playing Scrabble or going into town to see a movie.

That was our summer tradition, the rhythm of my life as a kid. There was nothing to think about. There was summer and what we did in the summer. It was simple.

It's not simple anymore.

I sit at the kitchen table, and Mom puts an apple juice pack in front of me without my asking. She pops a straw through it.

Mom says, "If you could go anywhere, where would you go?"

"I don't know," I say.

But I do know.

I'd go back in time.

I don't say that to Mom. It would freak her out.

I pull out the straw and squeeze the pack, watch a drop of juice dribble down the side.

Mom sniffles and turns away from me. She wipes a tear from her eye. She does it fast and dries her hand on her thigh like it didn't happen at all.

"It's a good idea, Mom. To have a vacation."

"You think so?" she says.

She smiles a little. That makes me feel better.

She says, "I had a crazy idea we might go to Europe. I've got some money saved up. It would be something different."

"Very different."

"Somewhere we've never been. A new experience."

"A new experience," I say. "Good idea."

Mom nods like she agrees, like we have a plan now.

But honestly, I don't think she'll do anything about it. Last summer we had this same talk. We planned a trip to California, talked about it for months, then stayed home. The plan dissolved, and we ended up stuck in New Jersey, both of us pretending it wasn't summer at all.

I WILL PURGE THY MORTAL GROSSNESS.

Later that night, I lie in bed with the Maglite next to me, staring at the ceiling.

I can't sleep. I've got too much on my mind.

The Maglite helps. I always have a flashlight in bed with me. If I wake up in the middle of the night, a night-light doesn't feel like enough. I need some powerful illumination. With a Mag, I can turn it on and it makes me feel safe. Police officers use Mags, too. Not only do the batteries last a long time, but the beam is bright and the flashlight itself is really heavy. You can blind a suspect, then whack him on the head. Perfect. You can even focus the lens by turning the head of the light.

That's what I do now. I point the beam up at the ceiling, make it fuzz out then focus back to a bright point.

I aim it at the closet. I think about the cardboard box

way up on the top shelf there, the one I haven't touched in a long time.

Dad's box.

It's brown cardboard, sealed with tape.

I remember sealing it and putting it up there.

I don't like to think about what's in it.

I take the light off the closet and move it back and forth on the wall, watch the beam shifting from place to place.

I hold it steady and look at the bright circle.

A spot.

The flashlight is like my own personal follow spot.

The idea is kind of funny.

I imagine how Josh would work a spot in the theater, swinging the light from girl to girl, laughing and waving when they looked up. And if Derek called for him, he would jog over to the ladder and slide down with a hand on either rail like a fireman going down a pole.

I wonder if I could work a spot like that.

I think about Derek's idea of using a follow spot. What if I were his op?

Spot op. That's what we call the job. *Op* is short for *operator*, the technician who runs the spotlight.

If I were spot op, the fairy girl would see me. Mr. Apple would know I could handle myself. And Derek?

He wouldn't be the only one who looked good.

I put the flashlight next to my head, feel the warmth of the beam on my cheek.

I imagine the fairy girl is next to me in bed. Maybe she's dressed, or maybe she's just wearing panties. I point the light at her, lift the sheet, and look at her body. Then I hand it to her and she points it back at me. We trade off like that, looking at each other in the light.

Looking and touching.

The room suddenly feels hot, and I kick off my blanket.

I take one last look at the fairy girl, then I turn out the light.

Just before I fall asleep, I think of the spotlight. Before it was just a nice idea. Now it seems like the answer to everything.

ASK ME NOT.

I'm walking backstage before rehearsal the next day when I see a big empty box from Times Square Lighting pushed into a corner. I run out to the stage and look to the back of the theater.

It's here.

A brand-new spotlight up on the catwalk, high over the audience's heads. It's a strange place for it because the position is a little too high, but I can see why they wouldn't take the time to build a special platform for it. Still, I don't know who set it up or if they knew what they were doing.

But I know it's here now.

And I want it.

I make my way into the audience where Derek and Ignacio are going over cues.

"Excuse me, Derek," I say.

"Well, well. The saboteur has emerged from his dark den," he says with a grin.

I can't tell if he's serious or making a joke, so I keep talking.

"I noticed a new spotlight on the catwalk," I say, "and I didn't see it on the light plot."

"That's because it wasn't there. I made an executive decision. With Mr. Apple's blessing of course."

"It looks new," I say, because that's very unusual for equipment at our level. For a public school, we have an impressive theater program. But our equipment is not exactly state of the art. More like state of decay. If we need something special for a show and there's enough in the budget, we might get a temporary rental. But then the best we can hope for is something that hasn't had the crap kicked out of it by a thousand other shows.

"It's brand-new," Derek says. "And it's ours to keep. A gift from an anonymous donor."

"Can you believe the luck?" Ignacio says.

Derek says, "It just so happens the donor shares a last name with yours truly."

He winks at me.

"Even luck can use a bit of assistance from my father," Derek says.

"So you're going to need an op."

I imagine my credit in the playbill:

ADAM ZIEGLER, SPOT OP.

I imagine the fairy girl reading my name and smiling.

"Why would I give you the spot when you mucked up my lights?" Derek says.

The actors pour into the theater, excited before their first walk-through.

"I'm already on lights," I say to Derek. "It kind of makes sense."

"It makes sense to you," Derek says. "Not to me."

"We have to get rolling," Ignacio says. "I've got twelve things to do and five minutes to do them in."

Derek doesn't say anything. He just lets me stand there, my face burning.

"Places!" Ignacio shouts.

I don't move.

"That includes you, Z," Ignacio says.

He points into the air.

REHEARSE MOST OBSCENELY AND COURAGEOUSLY.

Usually a walk-through is rough. The actors haven't worked on the set before, and they have to stop a lot to adjust blocking, their movements onstage. The first time on set, you expect it to go poorly.

But today is more like a disaster. Actors are forgetting their lines, stumbling over one another, breaking character. It looks like the first day of rehearsal rather than the next-to-last.

I see what Mr. Apple was talking about. The show looks bad.

I'm watching it all from the catwalk, where I can adjust lights or change gels as needed. I can also hear Mr. Apple at the tech table below, sighing as we hit one snag after another.

"Take the wash to seventy-five percent," Derek says. There's desperation in his voice, an intensity that's been increasing all afternoon as the rehearsal goes on.

Ignacio calls the adjustment, and the lights get brighter onstage.

Derek turns to Mr. Apple.

"This looks a lot better, doesn't it?" he says.

"Oh yes," Mr. Apple says. "Now I can see exactly what I've done to the American theater. And why I will never be forgiven."

Derek laughs like Mr. Apple is joking. Only I don't think he is.

"Miranda," Mr. Apple calls out to the stage. "Take a step stage left for me."

She moves and her face slips into shadow.

"What's going on over there?" Mr. Apple says to Derek.

Derek grabs a headset. "Take forty-seven to full," he says to Benno.

The lights in that area go to 100 percent, but there's still a dead zone, just like I saw on the lighting plot the other day.

"Who's on the catwalk?" Derek says into the headset.

"Me," I say.

"Who the hell is *me*?"

"Z," I say.

"You didn't focus stage left," Derek says.

"Yes, I did," I say.

"Have you looked at—why am I wasting my time? You can't climb down a ladder, much less hang a light."

"I hung everything according to the plot," I say.

"Of course you did," Derek says, his accent thickening.

Charming and insulting. His two specialties.

He leans over to Mr. Apple. "Our errant technician has struck again," he says. "But never fear. I have a solution. It's a perfect time to try our new spot."

"Fix it," Mr. Apple says. "I don't care how you do it."

"Mindy!" Derek shouts.

A cute little brunette jumps up from her seat in the back of the theater and runs onstage. I don't think I've ever seen her before.

"I want you on spot," Derek says to her.

"Anywhere you want me," she says with a big smile. She's wearing a miniskirt with tights underneath. Not exactly techie apparel. She starts to climb the ladder to the catwalk.

Grace is standing backstage, her eyes flitting back and forth from Mindy to Derek.

I'm starting to get a bad feeling about this.

I hear Mindy's footsteps, feel the tiny vibrations. She walks along the opposite side from me until she's out over the audience.

She moves towards the spot, looking at it like it's a foreign object.

You can tell a techie from a non-techie just by the way

they approach a machine. A techie approaches with fascination and curiosity, even if they have no idea how the thing works. A non-techie looks awkward, uncomfortable, out of place.

Just like Mindy.

If she's not a techie, what is she?

I look back at Grace. She's staring at Derek, looking hurt.

Mindy must be Derek's new girlfriend. DNF.

I key the mic on my headset. "Hang on, Mindy," I say. "I want to check out the spot before you work with it."

"I know what I'm doing," Mindy says. Her voice has a husky quality that makes me nervous.

Mindy throws some switches, but nothing happens.

"I'm serious," I say. "I'd like to give it a once-over."

Mindy manages to flip the correct switch. The power supply comes on and the fan hums to life.

"I told you I'm fine," she says. "Derek taught me everything."

I start towards her on the catwalk.

Below us onstage, Johanna and Miranda continue their scene.

MIRANDA

O, teach me how you look, and with what art
  You sway the motion of Demetrius' heart.

72

JOHANNA

I frown upon him, yet he loves me still.

"Standby on spot," Ignacio calls on the headset.

"Standing by," Mindy says.

"Ignacio, I want a minute with it before we go," I say.

"Stay out of it, Z," Ignacio says. "Derek set this up himself."

JOHANNA

The more I hate, the more he follows me.

MIRANDA

The more I love, the more he hateth me.

I hate Derek, so why should I care what happens with his spot?

It's not the spot, I realize. It's the show.

I care about the show.

"Make sure there's a gel on it," Derek says to Ignacio below.

"Derek wants it gelled," Ignacio repeats on the headset.

"Gel?" Mindy says. "Derek didn't teach me about that."

I click the headset mic.

"The color filter," I say. "Look for the handles on the top."

I'm a few steps away from her now, pointing with both hands.

Mindy looks frantic, pulling on different levers. She pulls the seventh lever and the entire set of gels pops out the top of the barrel.

"Which color?" she says.

"Spot go," Ignacio says.

Mindy holds the red button to make the spark, and a burst of white-hot light shoots out the end of the barrel.

"Now that's what I'm talking about!" Derek says.

I jump for her, trying to get to the spot.

MIRANDA

Love looks not with the eyes, but with the mind...

I'm too late. The unfiltered light shoots into Miranda's face, surprising her. Her hands go in front of her to block the light. She struggles to finish her line—

MIRANDA

...and therefore is wing'd Cupid painted blind.

—and she goes flying off the front of the stage, falling to the floor with a loud *crash*.

There's a gasp, followed by a scream, and then people are in motion, running towards the stage.

"House lights to full!" Ignacio shouts.

A second later I hear Miranda's voice from the pit in front of the stage:

"My leg!" she says.

"Oh my God," Mindy says in a tiny voice.

There's chaos below us, people crowding around Miranda, a first-aid kit open onstage, several people arguing about who called 911 first.

The spot is still on, the beam pointing straight up at the ceiling.

I reach past Mindy and flick off the light.

IS THERE NO PLAY?

The next twenty-four hours are chaos. Rumors fly, texts go back and forth, and everyone is calling everyone else and passing notes during class. First they say Miranda is okay, then they says she's in really bad shape, and there's even a point during the morning when people say Miranda died because she landed on a nail, which turned into an infection, which turned into a flesh-eating disease. That rumor is quickly squashed, but it's replaced with still more crazy rumors. Some of the techies are even betting on what the final diagnosis will be.

Finally Mr. Apple calls the cast and crew out of class for a meeting in the theater.

"I spoke with Miranda's parents not five minutes ago," Mr. Apple says when we're all assembled. "I hope this will dispel the rumors that are circulating."

The cast sits towards the front of the stage while the

crew hangs back. I'm standing in the door of the Cave, half in shadow, with Reach next to me.

"She's *not* dead," Johanna says. "I talked to her."

"You are correct," Mr. Apple says. "She is very much alive."

"I told you," Half Crack whispers next to me, and Benno passes him a five-dollar bill.

"But she has broken her leg," Mr. Apple says. "More than a break, really. A multiple fracture."

"Miranda!" Johanna cries out as if her friend just went down in a plane crash.

"What's the bad news?" Reach says.

I elbow him in the ribs.

"It's severe enough that she will be unable to continue in the show," Mr. Apple says.

He looks upset. He jams his fist into a bag of donuts, pulling out chunks of dough and pushing them into his mouth.

A wave of panic passes through me. What if the show is canceled? I imagine trying to get through the end of the school year without tech. There are only five weeks left, but five weeks without theater is like five years on a desert island.

"We're screwed," I say to Reach.

"Take it easy," he says.

No theater, followed by a long summer.

There's nothing easy about that.

"Couldn't she do it on crutches?" Johanna says.

"I was willing," Mr. Apple says, "but the doctor says it's not to be."

"What if she performs in a wheelchair?" Peter Mercurio says. Peter is the last of the four lovers, Lysander. Peter is gay, but you'd never know it unless he told you. He doesn't even seem like an actor, more like a baseball player who wandered into the theater by mistake.

"A wheelchair is impossible given our stage configuration," Mr. Apple says.

"How about on a computer monitor?" Derek says. "I could set up a multimedia platform onstage, and we could watch her performance on a laptop."

"All excellent ideas," Mr. Apple says. "None of them viable."

"Why isn't anyone talking about the techies?" Hubbard says. Hubbard is the short female actor who plays Puck. She's usually funny, but she doesn't seem funny right now. She points at us accusingly.

"This is all their fault. If they didn't screw up, Miranda would still be here."

"That's true," Peter says.

The actors turn and stare at us. At me in particular.

Why are they blaming me? I wasn't even the one on spot.

Reach steps in front of me, blocking their way.

"It's got nothing to do with us," Reach says. "That circuit board is a piece of crap."

"You mean the *dimmer* board," I whisper to him.

For a lighting guy, that would be an embarrassing mistake. Lucky for Reach, he doesn't have the embarrassment gene.

"The circuit board *and* the dimmer board! It's all crap!" he shouts.

"Then fix it," Johanna says. "We can't do it for you."

"We can't act for you," Benno says. "Why don't you fix your performance?"

"Why don't you fix your pants?" Jazmin says to Half Crack. "I've seen more of your ass than my baby brother's."

"Enough," Mr. Apple says. He stuffs a chunk of glazed donut in his mouth. "I've got plenty to worry about without these little catfights."

"Don't worry about a thing," Derek says to Mr. Apple. "We're going to act like professionals."

Derek points at the techies.

"Am I right, gentlemen?"

We nod. Reach grumbles next to me.

"What does it matter?" Johanna says. "We're screwed."

"It's going to be okay, honey," Wesley says.

"Are you a doctor?" Johanna says. "Can you fix her?"

Derek clears his throat.

"You mentioned there was good news, Mr. Apple. We could certainly use some."

"Indeed," Mr. Apple says. "The good news is that we're theater people, and theater people flourish in adversity. The show must go on."

"But how can it go on without Miranda? She's a lead," Peter says.

"We're going to have auditions," Mr. Apple says.

"We've got three more days," Johanna says. "That's not enough time for someone to learn the role."

"Exactly right," Mr. Apple says. "We need someone who is already a part of the show, knows the blocking, is familiar with the lines."

"Who?" Johanna says.

"One of the fairies," Mr. Apple says.

A stir goes through the cast.

I look for the girl from the hall. She's standing in the group of surprised fairies. She's dressed like a normal girl now—jeans, tank top, hair flattened down rather than wild.

"Mr. Apple, I'd like to address the techies if I might," Derek says.

"You have my blessing," Mr. Apple says. "And now, without further ado . . ."

Mr. Apple hefts himself up. He tucks Carol Channing under one arm and his bag of donuts under the other.

"I've got a date with a bag of donuts, and I don't want to disappoint."

He heads for the theater doors.

"Prepare yourselves, actors," he says over his shoulder. "We'll have auditions first thing in the morning."

He flings open the door, then looks back at the cast.

"Fate will smile on someone tomorrow," he says.

Carol Channing snaps at the bag of donuts and he pulls her back fast.

"That's not star behavior, Madam!" he says, and he goes out.

"Poor Miranda," Jazmin says.

"We should go to the hospital and visit her," Johanna says.

"Totally," Hubbard says. "We can bring her a cake or something."

"She loves chocolate," Johanna says. "Dark chocolate."

She bursts into tears. Wesley puts his arm around her, trying to comfort her.

"Come on, everyone," Peter says.

"I need to speak with the crew," Derek says. "I'll meet you there. And I'll pick up some flowers on the way."

"Thanks, Derek," Johanna says.

"Tech crew meeting in two minutes," he says.

The actors wander out into the house, while the techies head backstage.

I remember the fan is still running on the spotlight.

"I'll be right there," I tell Reach. "I have to turn off the spot."

I head for the ladder, and Johanna comes charging towards me.

"I know what you're up to," she says.

My mind goes through a rapid-fire list of things I might be guilty of. Looking down Miranda's shirt. Standing near the dressing room door with Benno last show so we could get a peak at actresses changing. Popping my zits on the catwalk even though there are people below.

"I saw you up there before Miranda fell," Johanna says.

"I had nothing to do with that. It was Mindy," I say.

"You were running towards the light."

"I was trying to stop her from making a mistake."

"I don't think so," she says. "I think you're trying to destroy the show. I saw *Phantom of the Opera*. I know how guys like you work. First the plan, then the mask, then the creepy stuff starts."

"Why would I want to destroy the show?"

"I don't know," she says. "Some weird techie vendetta."

"That's not true."

"I'm watching you. We all are."

She makes that motion, two fingers to her eyes, then one finger pointing at me.

We're watching you.

I AM SICK WHEN I DO LOOK ON THEE.

The entire tech crew stuffs itself into the Cave to wait for Derek. I look at the Techie Wall of Fame, covered with our pictures. I was proud when Reach got me onto the wall. I felt like I belonged. I had a purpose. It was two years ago, but it seems like another lifetime.

Derek strides in with a clipboard in his hands.

"Where's Mindy?" he says. He scans the room for the little spot op.

"Right here," she says, throwing him a big smile. "I'm really sorry—"

"You're off spot," Derek says.

"No way," she says.

"Yes way," he says, and turns his back on her.

Her face cracks and tears well up in her eyes.

"But you promised—" she pleads.

He spins around and shushes her like he's silencing a child.

I look across the room at Grace. She bites her lip.

Mindy jumps up and runs out of the room.

"That was harsh, dude," Half Crack says in a whisper.

Derek snaps him a look.

"Harsh. The entire tech program is about to go down the drain, and you think I'm being harsh?"

"I'm not the one who hired her," Half Crack says.

Derek steps back like he's been hit. I wince, waiting for him to attack. Instead he lifts his hands to the air like he's surrendering.

"Fair enough," Derek says. "I made an error in judgment. Even the best have their off days. But that's ancient history. The question before us now is: what's next?"

The room is silent.

"People are going to see this show. Important people," Derek says.

"Like your dad?" someone says under their breath.

"My father will be here to see my work. It's true. But think about what's at stake for all of us."

He paces the room, looking from face to face.

"It's not just my work up there. It's *our* work. The techie reputation is on the line. We may not be LaGuardia Arts, but damn it, we're Montclair. We can give them a run for their money!"

The faces in the room soften.

"I need your help to get us back on track. I can't do it without you, fellows."

It's quiet for a moment, and then Benno says, "We can't let it go down like this."

I notice a bunch of techies looking at Reach. Derek notices, too, because he says:

"What do you think, Mr. Patel?"

Reach leans back, crosses his arms.

"I think if this show goes down the crapper, it shouldn't be for technical reasons."

"I'm with you on that," Half Crack says.

Heads nod around the room.

"What are we going to do?" Ignacio says.

Reach stands up.

"I'll tell you what I'm going to do," he says. "I'm going to suck in my nuts and tech this mofo!"

The techies cheer.

"Brilliant," Derek says, patting Reach on the back.

Reach looks at me and shrugs his bony shoulders, like, *What else can we do?*

"Thank you so much, Rishekesh. That was quite inspiring," Derek says. "To begin, I need a new spot op. Someone who knows his business."

Grace's arm shoots up.

"I didn't realize you were still here," Derek says to her.

"I'm a techie," Grace says.

"Not for long," Benno whispers.

A few chuckles around the room.

"Any other volunteers?" Derek says.

Four or five hands rise.

Reach nudges me. I consider raising my hand, but I don't. Derek already knows I want it, and that all but guarantees he won't give it to me. Begging is just going to make it worse.

Derek studies the faces in the room.

"Let me think on it," he says. "And meanwhile, I ask you to think about how we can make this show better. Together."

The techies grunt their agreement. Derek heads for the door, pausing when he sees me.

I get this crazy thought that he's going to ask for my help. He'll put his arm around me and say, *We have to let bygones be bygones. I want you on my team, Z.*

"My beamer," he says.

"I haven't had a chance—" I say.

"I'm starting to wonder where your loyalties lie," he says, and he walks out.

"All right, everyone," Ignacio says. "Get a good night's sleep. There's going to be work to do in the next few days. Lots and lots of work."

He gets this wild, panicked look in his eyes and starts scribbling on a yellow pad.

"You'd better fill up that beamer," Ignacio says as he rushes by me.

"Better him than me," Half Crack says.

"Nobody wants to see you bending over and pumping gas," Benno says.

"Why not?" Half Crack says, oblivious.

The techies shuffle from the room. Grace grabs a chunk of wall next to me.

"I can't tell if Derek is evil or a genius," I say.

"I think he's an evil genius," she says. "But did you see me volunteer? And I hate him! Why would I volunteer?"

"Why would any of us?"

"That's the genius part," Grace says. "He makes people love him, too."

And then she moans like she has a stomachache.

Reach walks over, arms crossed. He looks from Grace to me.

"Do you know Grace?" I say.

"I know *of* her," he says.

Grace looks at the floor.

"She's good people," I say.

"Good at what?" he says.

He and Grace look at each other in a silent standoff.

"I'm going to bolt," she says to me.

"See you tomorrow," I say.

"So the rumor is true," Reach says when she's gone.

"What rumor?"

"The rumor I haven't told you about yet, but is somehow making you turn bright red. The one about you in the Cave with a certain girl."

"There was no girl."

"So Grace wasn't in there with you."

"She was there, but she's not a girl. I mean she's a girl, but I don't think of her that way."

Reach sighs, rolls up his sleeves.

"Don't get me wrong," Reach says. "Techie love is a beautiful thing. But not Grace. She's on our Do Not Call list."

"She kissed Derek. It's not like she has cancer."

"It's worse than cancer. She's infected with Derek. What if a speck of his spit is left inside her mouth, and you get too close and it sprays on you? It's like you had sex with Derek instead of her."

"They didn't have sex."

"How do you know? Because she told you they didn't? Forgive me, buddy, but you're a little naïve about these things."

Maybe Reach is right. But Grace is still my friend.

I say, "I don't think you should be criticizing Grace right now. At least not for sucking up to Derek."

"What does that mean?" Reach says.

"You gave him what he wanted."

"I didn't do it for him," Reach says. "I did it for us. For our reputation."

"If we look good, he looks good."

"Welcome to techie hell. Our entire job is to make someone else look like a star. Those are the rules of the game."

"Maybe I'm tired of the rules," I say.

"Let's discuss this on the walk home," Reach says.

"I still have work to do."

"But my mother is making chicken tikka," he says.

Reach thinks I love his mother's chicken tikka, probably because I always tell him I do. The truth is it gives me gas.

"Maybe we can walk together tomorrow," I say.

He sighs, gives me a little salute, and heads out.

I feel a pang in my chest. Reach and I used to walk home from rehearsal together every day. We'd talk about people, discuss tech theory, and plan our future conquests of girls and theater. Most of the time we'd get home then call each other again just to continue the conversation.

At some point we stopped doing that. It wasn't us. It was me. I was the one who stopped. I can't even remember when it happened. It's one of those weird relationship things—you never decide to do it, but it happens anyway. It's not until much later that you realize something changed. By then it's too late.

SINCE NIGHT
YOU LOVED ME.

Rehearsal is long over, and I'm still up in the catwalk. The house lights are at 50 percent. Even though the theater is huge, it feels intimate, like a room lit by candles.

The spotlight sits untouched out over the audience. I walk across the catwalk and stand behind it.

I grip the handles on both sides. I swing the metal, feel the mechanism swivel. Even though it's new, the side screw sticks slightly. It needs a shot of WD-40. I make a mental note.

"Hello!" I shout into the theater. "Anyone here?"

I'm alone. I flip the power switch on the light.

There's a humming sound as the fan comes to life, and then I press and hold the red button that sends a spark across the wires.

A beam of light shoots out the end of the spot and paints a hard circle on the stage floor.

It's like my Maglite, only on a giant scale.

I move the circle from side to side, pan up the wall and down again. I change the iris, shrinking and widening the beam. I do it fast and hard like a rock concert, then I do it smoothly like you would in a straight play.

I flip the spot up to the ceiling, look at it high in the air, then slash pan back down to the stage.

Someone is there.

It's the actress with black hair, standing alone in the center of the stage.

"Hello?" she says.

Sweat breaks out on my forehead.

"I know you're up there," she says.

I want to speak to her, but I have a real tendency to say the wrong thing when I talk to girls.

The best I can do is wag the light back and forth a little so she knows I heard her.

She looks up at me, cocks her head to one side.

Then she steps into the light.

Startled, I move the light off her, about two feet away to the side.

She puts her hands on her hips like she's pissed. Then she hops to the side, landing in the center of the light again.

I laugh. I can't help it. She looks so funny.

"I can hear you laughing," she says. "So I know you're not an alien."

I move the light away from her again. She slides to the right, keeping up with me. I move it forward and she moves forward, then I move it back and she moves back. Almost like we're dancing.

Dancing with light.

She looks up at me, holding her hands above her eyes so she can see.

"My name is Summer," she says.

"That's a strange name."

"Thank you very much."

"I didn't mean it like that. I guess I meant—I don't know how I feel about it."

"About my name? Why would you feel anything?" she says.

Summer. There are so many things I hate about summertime, so many that I love.

"I have issues with summer," I say. "It's a long story."

"Do you have issues with me?"

"I don't even know you."

"Good. Then we're starting from scratch."

I dim the light so it doesn't blind her.

"Are you the guy who almost killed Miranda?" she says.

"That's a lie."

"The actors believe there's some techie trying to kill them."

I think about what Johanna said. *I'm watching you.*

"Actors are crazy," I say.

"Look who you're saying that to. Actor," she says, raising her hand.

This is why I don't talk to girls. I make a mess of it.

"I'm sorry," I say. "I feel bad for Miranda. Really. It was a stupid mistake, but it wasn't my mistake. I just got blamed for it."

"Why you?"

"I'm the lighting guy. They always blame the lighting guy."

"Why?"

"The same reason they blame the techies. It's easy."

"Does the lighting guy have a name?" Summer says.

"Just lighting guy."

"That's kind of mysterious."

"You're the first girl in history to find techies mysterious."

"What are you talking about? James Bond is all about tech," she says. "He's pretty mysterious."

"He *uses* tech, he doesn't make it. He gets everything from Q. You don't see Q doing a lot of dating."

"Not on-screen. But off-screen he's a player."

"Is that right?"

"Oh yeah. James goes on a mission, and Q is sleeping with female spies two and three at a time."

I laugh.

"I know I'm not supposed to be in here," Summer says. "But I really need to practice for my audition. And it feels different standing on the big stage, you know?"

"I was practicing, too," I say.

"Maybe we can practice together."

I swing the spot towards her and pull focus so she's centered in the middle, head to toe in light.

She gives me the thumbs-up.

Her whole posture changes. Her shoulders slump, and she grasps at her stomach with one arm like she's exhausted and hurting. Then she does lines from the play:

SUMMER

Never so weary, never so in woe,
Bedabbled with the dew and torn with briers,

She kneels on the stage, her legs all but giving out beneath her. I focus in tighter so her body is wrapped in the light. At the same time I start to dim the spot.

SUMMER

I can no further crawl, no further go;
My legs can keep no pace with my desires.

I fade the spot further, changing the iris until the light

shrinks down to a circle on her face. She sighs, curls herself into a ball on the stage floor.

SUMMER

Here will I rest me till the break of day.

I fade the spot the rest of the way, dimming it until there's just a glow over her sleeping form. Then, in the silence, I click off the light. It makes a loud *snap* that echoes through the theater.

Summer kneels onstage looking up at me, her face partially in shadow.

One of Dad's paintings comes to mind. He called it *Woman Reclining at Night*. It's a large expanse of white and yellow with the barest hint of a woman lying off to one side, her skin nearly the same tone as the rest of the painting. It's like a pun on the idea of night, because instead of seeing nothing because of the dark, you see nothing because of the light.

I imagine what it would be like to go home and tell Dad about this girl, tell him how I thought about his painting when I was looking at her.

"Did my acting render you speechless?" Summer says.

"I was thinking about something else," I say.

"Not what an actor hopes for."

"Sorry. Your performance was great."

"I auditioned with that soliloquy, and I got cast as a fairy. So I suck," she says. "It's pretty obvious."

"You don't suck."

"I mean, I'm okay, but I'm not great. You know how there are some kids who get As and hardly do anything, and other kids who work super hard just to get a B? I'm the second kind."

"Wow. That's harsh."

I've never heard anyone who's as tough on themselves as I am.

"Harsh but true," she says. "Anyway, I can't do a Hermia speech. Johanna will kill me. I need a Helena speech, and I don't even know which one to do."

"Maybe you could do—" I stop myself.

"What were you going to say?"

"I'm not supposed to be talking to you," I say.

"According to whom?"

"You know."

"I don't know."

"There are rules about things like this," I say.

"Oh, that. Yeah, you guys are weird at this school. In my old school the actors got along with the crew."

"There's a lot of history here."

"What kind of history?"

"I don't know exactly. It's like the Hatfields and the McCoys. Someone stepped on someone's ballet slipper a hundred years ago, and we've been at war ever since. No one remembers why."

"It's kind of silly."

"Extremely," I say. "On top of that, there's the techie code."

"The code?" she says.

"We don't tell you how to do your job—"

"And we don't tell you how to do yours."

"No, you tell us, and we hate you and talk about you behind your back."

She laughs. "I need some help, mystery lighting guy. I give you permission to break the code."

The fan is whirring inside the spot. The vibration carries through the handles and into my palms.

If Reach were here, he'd kill me.

I look at Summer onstage, waiting for my help.

Reach on one side, Summer on the other.

"Anyway—" Summer says, starting to walk offstage.

"I was thinking about the speech 'Happy is Hermia,'" I say.

"Ah," she says, her face lighting up. She takes a breath, steps back, shakes out her hands. Her smile disappears.

SUMMER

Happy is Hermia, wheresoe'er she lies;
For she hath blessed and attractive eyes.

She pulls at her hair in frustration.

```
How came her eyes so bright? Not with salt tears:
  If so, my eyes are oftener wash'd than hers.
```

"I love that speech," she says. "It's sort of like, if crying made people beautiful, I would be the most beautiful girl in the world."

She smooths down her hair, white fingers running through black.

Beautiful.

"You must cry a lot," I say.

"All the time," she says.

She stops, thinks about it.

"Oh, I get it," she says. "Thanks for the compliment."

I'm sure I'm blushing. I'm glad she can't see me.

"Do you cry because you're sad?" I say.

"Sad, happy, frustrated. Lots of reasons."

"I guess it's okay for girls to cry."

"You don't cry?"

"Not for a long time."

Ignacio appears onstage dragging the ghost light behind him.

"Who are you talking to?" he says to Summer.

"The guy on the spotlight," she says.

"Nobody is supposed to be up there, not without my permission."

He looks up to the catwalk.

"Who's there?" he says.

"Hello," Summer says. "Lighting guy?"

"What his name?" Ignacio says.

"He didn't tell me his name."

"Answer me," Ignacio shouts up at me. "Chain of command!"

The spot has cooled down, so I click off the fan and run for it.

I hear Summer and Ignacio calling behind me, but I'm already gone, retreating on the catwalk, slipping down the backstage ladder, and disappearing into the shadows at the rear of the theater.

THE VILLAIN IS MUCH LIGHTER-HEEL'D THAN I.

I'm taking books out of my locker the next day when Reach comes up behind me.

"What's with the new black shirt?" he says.

"How can you tell it's new? I wear black every day."

"It's a slightly different shade of black."

"You're good," I say.

"There's a reason my job is called props *master*," he says. "So what's up?"

"Nothing's up."

"Interesting. Let me pass that through the bullshit detector." Reach sniffs the air and makes a face. "You failed."

"Give me a break."

"Let's start with that wannabe techie yesterday. What's her name again?"

"Grace. And she's not a wannabe."

100

"You're into her, aren't you?"

"No."

Reach sniffs the air.

"Okay, fine," I say. "There is somebody I like. But it's not Grace."

"Who?"

"You don't know her," I say.

I barely know her.

"I know everyone with breasts," Reach says.

"She doesn't go to our school."

"My radar extends for a seventy-five-mile radius," Reach says. "That makes me a threat throughout the tri-state area."

Summer comes around the corner, walking right towards us. She's wearing shorts with white cutoff socks that make her legs look very long.

"We'll talk about it later," I say.

"And you'll tell me everything?"

Summer is getting closer and closer.

"I'll show you a friggin' video," I say. I push Reach towards his classroom. "But later. I don't want you to be late for class."

"How sweet. You're worried about me," Reach says. He takes a step into the classroom, then turns back.

"Don't forget to put gas in Derek's car," Reach says.

"Okay, Mom," I say.

Reach looks hurt. "I'm trying to help you," he says. "You don't want to take Derek down, so you're going to have to build him up. It's one or the other. I don't make the rules, so don't bust my balls about it."

He slips into the classroom just as Summer walks up.

I want to say something to her, but when she gets close, I chicken out and turn around like someone called me from down the hall. I hold my breath, waiting for her to pass by.

Only she doesn't.

"Excuse me," she says. "Were you in the hall yesterday?"

I turn around like I'm surprised.

"When?" I say.

"When I was dancing."

"You were dancing in the hall? That's kind of strange."

"Sorry, I thought it was you," she says.

"It wasn't," I say, hating myself even as the words come out of my mouth.

"You look like a theater guy," she says.

"I'm not a theater guy. I'm a *techie*."

"But you're not *that* techie."

"The one in the hall? No. I don't hang out in halls."

"You're in the hall now," she says.

"I'm in it, but I'm not hanging out in it. I'm just passing through it."

The first bell rings. Students speed up around us.

She says, "It's just . . . Someone helped me out yesterday, and I wanted to thank him."

Derek comes strolling around the corner. He's wearing one of those pageboy caps, whistling, and walking like he owns the place.

"It wasn't me," I say to Summer, and I head in the opposite direction.

"Whatever," she says behind me, sounding a little pissed.

I don't blame her. I'm an idiot.

I nod as I pass by Derek. At first he looks at me like he's never seen me before, then he stops.

"You—" he says like he's trying to come up with my name.

"Z," I say.

"I remember now. I have something for you, Z."

"For me? What is it?"

"A bit of Tennyson." He recites: "'I must lose myself in action, lest I wither in despair.'"

"What is that?"

"It's how I live my life," Derek says.

"Very interesting," I say, which is what we say in the theater when something is not interesting at all. For example, if your friend does tech for a bad play and then asks if you liked it, you say, *It was interesting*.

"You don't get it, do you?" Derek says.

"I guess not."

103

"Translation: If you want something, go for it. Or else you'll spend your life thinking about it."

"I see," I say, which is another thing we say in the theater when we don't see at all.

The second bell rings and the last few stragglers rush off to class.

"You have to ask yourself what you want," Derek says.

He reaches into his pocket and takes out his BMW keys.

"And what are you willing to do to get it?"

I stare at the keys.

He says, "I could have gotten rid of you after the spotlight incident. The actors wanted me to. They've got some crazy idea that you're trying to sabotage the show."

"That's not true," I say.

"Of course not," Derek says. "I told them it was ridiculous. But rumors have this nasty habit of reviving themselves. Unless, of course, one is diligent about squashing them."

A light flickers overhead. The hall is empty now except for the two of us.

"Never fear," Derek says. "I've got your back."

"Why?"

"Because I've got plans for us."

"What kind of plans?"

"First things first," he says.

He dangles the BMW keys in front of me.

The hall lights are glinting off the metal.

I think about Summer. I think about being the spot op, lighting her night after night.

I think about how she looked onstage, smiling up at me, running her fingers through her hair.

Pull him down or build him up. That's what Reach said.

I take the keys.

"Good man," Derek says.

LOOK, HERE COMES HELENA.

When I walk into the theater that afternoon, the cast is milling around onstage, chattering and whispering. I slide into the wings without being seen.

Grace pops out of the curtain behind me.

"What's up?" she says.

"You scared me," I say.

"Hey, you're not the only techie with invisibility skills."

"It's not that I don't want to talk to you," I say. "But Reach heard I was in the Cave with you. He's on my case in a big way."

I scan the backstage area.

"Yeah, I'm real scary." She holds her arms out in front of her. "Beware Frankentechie. She crushes young techies and throws them into the river."

"I'm serious, Grace."

"Okay, okay. I'll play it cool."

She shrinks back so she's hidden in shadow.

I look at the actors waiting onstage. Summer is in the rear of the group, hanging back with the fairies.

"Why are the actors out here?" I ask Grace.

"They had auditions. They're waiting for the Big Apple to announce his decision."

"That's exciting."

"Maybe if you're an actor," she says. "For me it's a yawnfest. Pick someone and let us stuff her into a costume and get back to work."

She rolls her eyes, and I laugh.

"Don't let Reach see you laughing. On pain of death!" she says.

I'm starting to like Grace despite myself.

Mr. Apple shuffles out to the front of the stage, and the actors surge forward.

Summer stays in the back. I see the anxiety on her face.

Derek's voice pops into my head. *"I must lose myself in action,"* he said.

The last thing I want to do is take advice from Derek, but looking across the stage at Summer, I think he's right. I have to act.

There's no chance Summer is going to get the part, not when she's up against more experienced actors who have paid their dues. I imagine she'll be heartbroken after the announcement. She'll turn to me with tears in her eyes, and I'll comfort her. She'll thank me and fall into my arms.

"I'll be right back," I tell Grace.

Mr. Apple says, "I want to thank everyone for reading for the role on such short notice."

I move up behind Summer.

"I think I'm going to throw up," she says to the fairy next to her.

"We had an excellent round of auditions," Mr. Apple says, "but one actor stood out from the pack."

Summer senses me behind her and turns. She looks confused.

"You—" she says.

"I want to tell you something," I say.

"Summer Armstrong!" Mr. Apple says.

Summer looks up when she hears her name. Actors pull at her, dragging her towards the front of the stage.

It all happens in slow motion like that scene in that movie when everything goes wrong and you can't stop it.

"It's me?" she says.

"Congratulations," Mr. Apple says. "You're the new Helena."

The actors burst into applause.

I walk back to Grace.

"What was that about?" she says.

"My brilliant plan," I say. "Which turned out to be not-so-brilliant."

I look at her in the front of the stage, surrounded by actors.

"She's a lead. I'll never be able to talk to her now."

Grace looks at me, surprised.

"Are you crushing on an actor?" she says.

I grab her arm and pull her deeper into the wings.

"Don't say anything. You have to promise me."

"Okay, okay," she says. "I'm just a little shocked. I didn't know you were a rebel."

"I'm not a rebel."

"You're talking to me, you're crushing on an actor . . . Face it. You're the techie Che Guevara."

I think about that for a second, the possibility that I'm getting more courageous. Then I look at Summer basking in the applause. I've run away from her three times now.

I'm not courageous at all. Not without a spotlight in front of me.

"I give up on girls," I say. "I'm going to join the priest-hood."

"Aren't you Jewish?" Grace says.

I slump down to the floor.

Something digs into my thigh. I tap my pocket and feel Derek's BMW keys.

I take them out.

"Those look like Derek's keys," Grace says.

"He gave them to me."

"Wow. Nobody gets to touch that car," she says. "He made me put a towel down before I sat in it, and that's when he was going out with me."

"I'm supposed to put gas in it."

"Do you want me to show you where he parks it?"

Grace and I go out to the parking lot. She leads me to the back corner where Derek's red convertible is angled across two spaces so no other cars can get near it.

"I have to admit it's a beautiful car," I say.

"Everything Derek has is nice," Grace says.

"Except his ego," I say. "I'm going to take it around the corner and put gas in the tank."

"Do you have a license?" Grace says.

"Learner's permit."

"Don't get pulled over."

"No kidding. That would suck."

I unlock the car and get in. I look down at the gearshift.

"Problem: I don't drive stick."

"You're a techie," she says. "How could you not drive stick?"

"My dad was supposed to teach me," I say.

"Why didn't he?" she says.

I don't feel like talking about it now, so I say:

"Plans change. You know."

"Dads suck," Grace says. "Mine is on me like a barnacle."

I look down at the gearshift, wondering how far I can get by faking it.

Not far, I decide.

"What am I going to do about the car?" I say.

"Move over," Grace says. "I can drive anything with wheels."

I AM AMAZED AT YOUR PASSIONATE WORDS.

I'm sitting in Derek's convertible with the top down as Grace slams the car through a series of shifts that make the engine roar.

"This doesn't suck, huh?" she says.

"Not at all," I say.

I have to shout to be heard over the wind.

"Maybe you should slow down a little," I say.

I think how Mom would freak out if she was in a car going this fast. Especially a convertible. What happens if you flip over in a convertible? There's nothing there to protect your head. Anything could happen.

"I'm serious. Slow down," I say.

"Relax," Grace says. "I've been driving since I was twelve. My grandfather used to let me drive his Honda in the church parking lot on Sundays. And he learned in the Philippines where they have no traffic rules."

She winks at me, but I don't find it funny.

"You're really scared, aren't you?" she says, and she slows down a little.

"Not scared," I say.

"It's okay," she says. "We should keep it under the speed limit anyway."

She eases back on the gas and I relax, even putting my hand outside of the car so I can feel the air buffeting my fingers.

"I've been wondering about something," Grace says. "Why did you talk to me that first time?"

"I felt bad for you."

"But why? You didn't even know me."

"You were crying. I guess it reminded me of someone."

"Your girlfriend?" Grace says.

"I don't have a girlfriend."

"What about that actor?"

"What about her?" I say.

Grace slams gears and my head jerks back.

"Sorry about that," she says.

She pulls a hard U-turn into the gas station.

"Who did I remind you of?" she says.

"My mom."

"Oh," she says.

She looks straight ahead.

"Is it because I'm fat?" she says.

"My mom is thin," I say. "And so are you."

"I'm techie thin. Not actor thin."

"What's the difference?"

"Fifteen pounds."

"I like how you look, Grace."

I study Grace in the late-afternoon light. Her skin is the color of roasted almonds. I think about how I would light her if she were onstage. With Summer, you have to add color because she's so pale. With Grace, I would highlight the color that's already there.

At the gas station we wait for a truck to finish so we can pull up to the pump.

"That actress is much thinner than me," Grace says.

"That actress doesn't even know my name," I say.

"Do you want her to?"

"I guess so. Why not?"

"The techie rules. You're the one who told me about them."

"I'm starting to wonder if they're techie rules or Reach's rules."

"Either way you'd be breaking them."

"That's true," I say. "And I'm not much of a rule breaker. Despite what you think."

"Love makes you do crazy things," she says. "I know better than anyone."

She pulls up to the pump and kills the engine.

"You know what? I'm not sure that girl deserves to know your name. Maybe you're too good for her."

"Maybe you're too good for Derek," I say.

She grins, flips hair from her eyes.

"Do you think so?" she says.

I nod.

"Thanks, Adam," she says.

"Let's gas this thing up and dump it back at school."

"Deal," she says.

Ten minutes later, we pull into the school parking lot. As we drive in, I glance in the side mirror and see a flash of someone coming out the back door of the school.

"Here comes Derek!" I say.

Grace pulls behind a truck and jams the car into park.

"Switch with me!" she says.

She unbuckles and jumps up on the seat.

She slides over the gearshift as I struggle to unhook my leg from under her. She turns to let me get by, and the side of her breast brushes my face.

"Awkward," she says.

"Super awkward," I say.

I scurry over the gearshift and plop into the driver's seat, both of us laughing like crazy as Derek walks up.

"Why did you park all the way back—" Derek says.

He stops when he sees Grace.

"Why is she in my car?" he says.

Grace starts to say something, but I interrupt her.

"I made her come with me," I say.

"Why?" Derek says.

"I've got a learner's permit. I need an adult with me."

"She's not an adult," Derek says.

"Cops don't know that," I say. "They just see two people in the car."

Grace starts giggling. I give her an elbow in the ribs.

Derek looks at us. "What's going on between you two?"

"Nothing," I say.

"I just love your beamer," Grace says, taunting him.

"We all love the beamer," I say, trying to sound authentic.

Derek steps back and crosses his arms.

"Something's different about you," he says to Grace.

Grace stops laughing.

"Different how?" she says.

"Did you get your hair cut?"

Her hand jumps to her hair, smoothing it down in back.

"Yes," she says.

"It looks good," Derek says. He smiles.

Grace turns red. "Thank you," she says.

Derek looks back at me. "I appreciate you taking care of my baby," he says.

The way he says it, I can't be sure if he's talking about

the car or Grace. I sense her squirming in the seat next to me.

I hop out and pass Derek the keys.

"Twelve gallons of super. On me," I say.

"I won't hear of it," Derek says. He pulls out a wad of bills and peels off two twenties. "You don't have to pay for me. I just wanted to see how serious your commitment to the team was."

"Serious," I say.

"You're an interesting chap," Derek says. "More interesting every time I speak with you."

He starts to walk away, then stops.

"Have you ever worked a follow spot?" he says.

"I have," I say.

"I hoped you would say that."

He winks at me, throws Grace a brief smile, and heads back towards school.

He makes it about ten feet when he holds the key fob over his head and presses. The car lets out a loud *honk* that makes Grace and me jump.

Derek waves without turning and disappears into the school.

"What the hell just happened?" I say.

"Derek happened," Grace says.

WE SLEEP, WE DREAM.

The actors are running scenes onstage as I climb to the catwalk and take my official place behind the spot. I slide the iris lever, pull the motorcycle grips that control focus. I flip gels in and out, getting a feel for the light again.

I'm the spot op, I think.

And all it cost me was a half hour to put gas in Derek's car.

It's a small trade-off. Help Derek, and he helps you.

It seemed like such an awful thing before, but now that I've done it, it feels easy, even natural.

But then I think of Grace and Mindy, other techies who have been in Derek's good graces. I think about what happened to them afterwards.

I'm different. That's what I tell myself.

For one thing, I'm not a girl.

For another, I'm careful. Super careful.

Which means I'm going to be okay.

I pop the color boomerang and look through the gels that Derek has selected. The colors are rudimentary. Red, Blue, Green, Yellow.

Green makes you look like a monster. Red is passion. Yellow is day. Blue is night. All the color clichés.

Summer is not a cliché. She's special. She needs a special light. I think about her hair, her skin tone. All the ways light could bring out the qualities I see in her.

I've got some sheets of gel nearby, nothing on Derek's plan, just colors I like. I pull my utility knife and slice out a circle of pale amber. I hold it in front of my eyes, look at the stage through it.

I slide out Derek's red gel and replace it with the amber.

It feels like I'm helping him. I'm on his team now, so I'm doing something to make the team better.

"Could we try the spot there?" Derek says in the house below.

"In the middle of the scene?" Mr. Apple says.

Derek lowers his voice so the actors can't hear. But I'm above him, so I hear it all.

"The scene is a little boring," he says to Mr. Apple. "This might spice it up."

"You have a point," Mr. Apple says. "We need as much spice as possible."

Derek signals to Ignacio, Ignacio to Benno.

I hear Ignacio's voice on headset. "Let's get the spot up," he says. "It's all you, Z."

"Will do," I say.

I flip on the power supply, feel a thrill as the fan whirs to life inside the metal casing. I bend over, using the sight to aim where the beam will appear.

"Spot ready," I say.

"Actors, stand by for spot," Ignacio says. He's being extra careful because of what happened to Miranda.

"Spot go," Ignacio says.

I hold down the red button, wait for the spark to catch and fire across the gap. It takes less than a second for light to shoot from the end of the barrel.

Summer's face is enveloped in a soft glow as if lit by candlelight. The effect is subtle to the audience, obvious to me. The wide, flat picture onstage now has dimension and intimacy.

Summer looks at Wesley with love in her eyes.

SUMMER

And I have found Demetrius like a jewel,

Mine own, and not mine own.

Only in my mind, she's not talking to Wesley. She's talking to me. I'm onstage with her, the two of us standing together in the light. She reaches for me . . .

WESLEY

Are you sure

That we are awake?

Wesley puts his arms around Summer. That snaps me back to reality.

I'm nowhere near the stage, nowhere near Summer.

I'm not the one who gets the girl; I'm the one who lights her.

So that's what I do.

I pull the lever to slide a gel into the spot. Not just any gel. The amber one. The special color I chose.

A subtle rose hue blooms on Summer's cheeks. Now she is even more beautiful in Wesley's arms.

"Stop!" Derek shouts. "What's going on up there?"

"I'm having a great time," Wesley says, squeezing Summer hard against him.

Johanna's fist clenches, ready to punch him.

"I mean up *there*," Derek says, pointing to my spot.

I don't say anything.

Derek races over to the tech table and grabs the headset out of Ignacio's hands.

"What is that color, Z?"

"I was trying something," I say.

"Oh, you were trying something," he says. "Thank you so much for your input, but it won't be needed."

121

"I thought you might like it."

"I like my light plot," Derek says. "I'd appreciate if you would do your job and accomplish it for me."

"I like this light," Mr. Apple says.

Derek holds his hand over the mic.

"You mean you like the spot," Derek says to him.

"I mean the *color* of the spot," Mr. Apple says.

Derek holds his hand over his ear like he's listening to something on the headset. Which is strange, because I'm not saying anything.

"Oh, that's right," Derek says like he's speaking to me. "I did make that change. Thanks for reminding me, Z."

He turns to Mr. Apple.

"Glad you like it," Derek says. "That's the new Act Four color."

Mr. Apple raises one eyebrow.

"Excellent choice," he says.

"Indeed," Derek says. He hands the headset back to Ignacio.

"Well done then," Mr. Apple says.

"You've got to be kidding me," Reach says in my ear.

THE MOST
LAMENTABLE COMEDY.

"You got robbed," Reach says in the Cave during the break. "I can't believe it. He took credit for your work."

I shrug.

"No reaction? Righteous indignation? Nothing?"

"I got the light into the show. That's what's important."

"Who are you, Lighting Board Gandhi? On a selfless mission to bring light to the untalented?"

"I'm thinking big picture."

"I'll tell you the big picture: you got shafted, and I don't like it. You're my boy. I'm supposed to protect you."

"I don't need protecting."

"What does that mean?"

"Nothing," I say.

"It doesn't sound like nothing. It sounds like you've got something on your mind."

I imagine telling Reach how I feel. But I'm not even sure what I would say.

So I change the subject.

"The car thing was a good idea," I say. "It got me the spot job."

Reach looks at me, suspicion on his face. Then he smiles.

"Admit it. I've still got it," he says.

"You've got something."

"I've got *it*. Genius. Evil-plan genius."

"You've got it," I say.

Reach wipes a fake tear from the corner of his eye.

"I love tech," he says. "Where else can you get this kind of male bonding in high school?"

"Sports," I say.

"Sports guys have to shower together," Reach says. "Which is not cool in any way, shape, or form."

Something large blocks the light in the doorway. It's Mr. Apple. He stands there cradling Carol Channing.

"Mr. Apple, we don't often see you backstage, sir," Reach says.

"If you're going to kiss my ass, Mr. Patel, it's a large-scale undertaking."

Reach clears his throat.

"Well, the props table isn't going to reset itself," Reach says, and he slips out the door.

Mr. Apple enters the Cave. "Was it you who changed the gel?"

What do I tell him? I could throw Derek under the bus like he did to me after the blackout. But why risk it? I'll gain an enemy in Derek, and maybe have a small chance of impressing Mr. Apple.

"It wasn't me," I say. "It was on the light plot. Derek just forgot."

Mr. Apple nods and scratches Carol Channing's head. We stand there for a while, so long that I start to feel uncomfortable.

"I think the show is going better," I say.

"It's a disaster," Mr. Apple says.

He starts to breathe hard, his chest rising and falling. He slips a hand into his pocket and I hear paper crinkling.

"My paper bag," he says. "Better to have and not need than need and not have."

He holds a finger to his nose and makes a *shhhhh* sound.

"Our secret," he says.

"Mr. Apple, things are usually bad during tech, aren't they? But they get better when the show gets closer to opening."

"In most circumstances that is the case."

"You don't think it's going to happen this time?"

"You don't understand. It's not just the acting or the design. It's me."

"What about you?"

"I'm losing it," he says. He holds his hands over Carol Channing's ears. "Not that I ever had it to begin with. I'm not a director. I'm a failed actor. I've just been faking it in Montclair High School for fifteen years. Most people have career trajectories. Mine is like an oil rig. Straight down."

"I think you're a good director," I say.

"And you're basing that on what? Your years of professional experience?"

I look at the ground.

"I'm sorry," Mr. Apple says. "Forgive me, lad. I'm more worried than Julie Taymor in a hospital waiting room."

"What are you worried about?" I say.

"What do you see when you look at that stage?"

"I see light. What do you see?"

"I see disaster waiting to happen," Mr. Apple says.

"But light can make the show better."

"Is light that powerful?" he says with a grin.

"To me it is."

Mr. Apple sighs. "I need a little of what you have, lad."

"What do I have?"

"Youthful naïveté."

"You're still young," I say.

"I'm forty-three years old," Mr. Apple says. "That's one hundred and seven in gay years."

"But you can still fix the production," I say.

"I'm somewhat lacking in inspiration right now. It's what's known as *phoning it in*."

"You mean you're not trying."

"I'm trying to try," Mr. Apple says. "You have experience with that?"

I think about life since Dad died. The way it feels empty, but it keeps going anyway. And I have no choice but to keep going with it.

Trying to try.

"I do," I tell Mr. Apple.

"Isn't that interesting," Mr. Apple says.

He holds Carol Channing in one hand and swings her back and forth like she's flying. She yelps and kicks her little legs, but I can't tell if she's terrified or enjoying the adventure.

"It sounds like we're both in need of inspiration," Mr. Apple says.

"Where do we find it?"

"Discover that," Mr. Apple says, "and you've solved one of life's great mysteries."

TRUST ME, SWEET.

I step out the backstage door into the theater department hallway. Derek is there, leaning against the wall, waiting for me.

"Do me a favor, would you, Z?"

"What is it?"

"Take the knife out of my back."

Was Derek eavesdropping? Did he hear what Mr. Apple said to me?

"Is this how you repay a kindness?" he says. "I put you on spot. I *entrust* you. And what do you do? You change my lighting plot."

"That was a mistake," I say, secretly relieved. I'm still in trouble; I'm just in trouble for something else.

"So the gel changed itself?" Derek says.

"No, it was me. I was testing something out, and I forgot to put it back. I'm sorry."

"It's little mistakes like that which have me reconsidering your position in the grand scheme of things," he says.

"It worked out pretty well for you," I say.

Derek raises one eyebrow.

"Is that a challenge?" he says.

I didn't mean to challenge him; it just popped out. Is that what courage does?

I always thought you had to decide to be courageous, but what if I was wrong? What if courage is just a reflex like fear, and it can come out anytime it wants to?

Anything could happen.

"You're upset because I took credit for the color of the spot. Is that it?" Derek says.

"A little. Yes."

"You feel like I stole it from you."

"I didn't say that."

"Well, guess what? I did steal it," Derek says. "You work for me now. If I look good, you look good. That's what it means to work for someone, to be a team player. We rise or fall together."

Derek's speech is so convincing, I almost believe him. ut something bothers me about his idea. If he takes credit for people's successes, shouldn't he take the blame for their mistakes? That's not what he did after the blackout.

Then again, I wasn't on his team then. Maybe things are different when you're on the team.

"Rise or fall," I say.

"That's right," Derek says. "Speaking of rising, how do you like being on spot?"

"I like it," I say.

"And you're good at it. Even better."

"I love light," I say, and immediately wish I hadn't. "That sounds pretty stupid, doesn't it?"

"It doesn't sound stupid at all. Remember who you're talking to. I'm a designer," Derek says.

He glances both ways down the hall to see if we're alone.

"You know what I love?" he says. "Fog."

"Like in London?"

"Stage fog. You hit it from the side with a bank of light—*boom*. Instant mood. I'm thinking we should do *Wicked* as the spring musical next year, just so I can fog the hell out of everything."

"That would be fun," I say.

"No kidding," Derek says. "Lights, fog, a strobe, a couple flash pots. We'd blow these people's minds."

"Like high-school theater on steroids."

"Now you're getting the idea," Derek says. "So I can count on you, right? You've got my back with Apple?"

"I do," I say.

He gives me a wink, then starts to go.

"Incidentally," he says, "that girl, Grace—she's quite a character, isn't she?"

"What do you mean?" I say.

"Don't believe everything she tells you," he says.

He studies me for a minute.

"What did she tell you?" he says.

"Nothing."

"Just in case, I want you to hear it from the horse's mouth. We went out a couple times. That much is true. But my God, she acts like we were married or something. You know how women are," he says.

"I know," I say, even though I don't know.

"Point is I want you to stay away from her. She's not techie material. We need to get rid of her before we have another Mindy incident."

I think Derek has it wrong. I've watched Grace building sets the last two days, and she's better than most carpenters. She might even be the best I've seen.

"Are you with me on this?" Derek says.

I check the hall, hoping someone will come along and end the conversation. But there's nobody.

Derek is standing a foot away, waiting for my answer.

"I'm with you," I say.

THOUGHTS AND DREAMS AND SIGHS.

I go upstairs to the third floor to get my books out of my locker.

I think about what I said to Derek. Am I really with him now?

The whole thing is confusing.

I throw my backpack over my shoulder and head downstairs to the front of the school. I need some time to think, and there's less chance of running into anyone if I go out the front.

"Wait up!" Grace calls.

Less chance. But still a chance.

"What are you doing in front?" I say.

"Avoiding Derek. What are you doing?"

"Avoiding everyone."

"Can I walk with you?"

"I need to think."

"You can't think and walk at the same time?"

She smiles at me.

"Come on," I say.

And we walk out together.

It's past eight and traffic is light. We walk for a couple blocks in silence.

"I smell smoke," Grace says, tapping my head.

"I've got a lot on my mind."

"You want to talk about it?"

"I don't know."

"I cried and blew snot on your shoulder," Grace says. "I think I owe you one."

"Were you really Derek's girlfriend?" I say.

"What kind of question is that? You saw me crying over him."

"Girls cry for a lot of reasons."

"I don't believe this," Grace says. "What did he tell you?"

"How do you know he told me anything?"

"Because I know him. He's like the devil. Only with better cologne."

"He said it was never serious between you."

"I hate guys," she says. "I swear to God."

We cross the street together. Grace picks at a zit on the side of her nose.

"Take it easy," I say. "You'll make it bleed."

She stops walking.

"Do you believe him?" she says.

I look at the place under her chin where she showed me the mark. It's faded, but it's still there.

"No," I say.

"Good."

"But things are really confusing right now," I say. "I'm getting pulled in a lot of directions."

I think about my last year of junior high when Josh gave me a tour of the high school. He didn't want to, but Dad kind of forced him. We walked through the halls and Josh introduced me to everyone, and after they passed by, he gave me their status—who was in, who wasn't, people you had to avoid, and the ones you should get closer to. He said it like it was obvious, but I couldn't see any of that by looking at them.

When I asked Dad about it later, he said Josh was obsessed with stuff like that, and I should do my best to ignore it.

"If you get into that mindset, it never ends," Dad said. "Even when you're an adult. I can measure myself against every painter in the world, living and dead, and what does it get me?"

I wanted to believe Dad was right, but I couldn't deny that Josh had some secret knowledge that I didn't have. I just wasn't sure if you needed knowledge like that to be successful in high school.

Right now it feels like you do.

Am I a techie?

Derek's flunky?

A rebel?

If I talked to Josh, maybe I wouldn't be so confused. We could sort it out together.

"Are you still with me?" Grace says.

"I'm here," I say. "Just thinking about things."

"I have to stop at Enzo's and pick up a pizza for my mom," Grace says. "How about if I distract you with some Italian food?"

"Will that solve all my problems?"

"You've got two choices: a slice or Ritalin."

"I'll take a slice. We'll leave the Ritalin for Ignacio."

SPEAK THOU NOW.

Enzo's is the pizza place down the street from school. It's like a giant Italian restaurant cliché—red plastic tablecloths and a wall of old wine bottles stacked in rows—but the food is really good. During the day kids come here to get a slice for lunch, but in the evening it's a whole different crowd, families from the neighborhood and couples on dates.

And techies.

When I walk in, the crew is sitting around a big table, laughing and talking loudly with pizzas in front of them. I start to back up, but it's too late. Reach sees me.

He jumps out of his seat and rushes over, a huge smile on his face.

"You made it out!" he says. "To what do we owe the honor?"

He looks over my shoulder. Grace is ordering at the front counter.

The smile disappears.

"What am I seeing?" Reach says. "Are you on a date?"

"It's not a date. I told you I'm not interested in her."

"Then what's she doing here?"

"She's getting her mom something," I say.

"Not cool, dude."

Grace sees us and waves.

"Please be nice to her," I say. "She'll make a great techie."

"Is it that important to you?" Reach says.

Before I can answer, Grace walks up.

"Hi, Reach," she says.

Reach looks at me, upset.

"The crew is here getting some food," I tell Grace.

"Are you going to stay?" Grace says.

"I guess I will," I say. "Want to sit down with us for a minute, Grace? While you wait for your pie?"

She looks to Reach. He forces a half smile.

"Whatever," he says, and goes back to the techie table.

"Forget it," Grace says. "He doesn't want me here."

"He wants you. He just doesn't know it yet. None of them do."

"I don't want to cause trouble," Grace says.

"We're already here," I say. "Let's go break the ice."

I drag Grace to the table where the techies are in mid-conversation.

"Hey, guys," I say. "You know Grace, right?"

Nobody says a word.

"Pull up a couple chairs," Reach says.

That eases the tension a bit. I sit down and put Grace next to me.

"We're playing Worst Accidents," Benno says, bringing me up to date. "I was just talking about a time my screwdriver went into an electrical outlet."

"One-ten volt?" Half Crack says.

"Yeah," Benno says.

"Ha! That's nothing," Half Crack says. "Once I was working on my mom's dryer, and I went right into the two-twenty line by mistake."

"Did it get you?" Reach says.

"Sure did. And let me tell you, you feel that shit. When I came to, I was lying across the room with all the hair standing up on my arm."

"What about your johnson?" Reach says.

"That did not stand up," Half Crack says.

"I was referring to pubic hair," Reach says. "If all the hair on your body reacts, it stands to reason that your pubic hair would, too."

"You're assuming he has pubic hair," Grace says.

"Whoa," Benno says.

The table goes silent.

"Maybe you didn't get the memo," Half Crack says to

her, "but I'm known for my pubes. I've got a long-haired dachshund between my legs."

"You're sure it's not one of those Egyptian dogs?" Grace says. "You know, the little bald ones?"

"Slam!" Benno says.

The techies laugh.

"I like this girl," Benno says.

Half Crack gives her a dirty look, but then he laughs, too.

"You're pretty tough," he says.

"Of course I'm tough. I'm a techie," Grace says.

That earns a roar of agreement from the guys. This is going better than I had hoped.

The waitress brings a fresh pizza, and the techies dig in.

"Hey Z, when's the last time you came out with us?" Benno says.

"A month maybe?" I say.

"It's been, like, a year," Reach says.

"No way."

"You've been very standoffish since you got leprosy," Reach says.

Could it be a whole year? I try to remember the last time I was out so I can prove to Reach that it wasn't so long ago. I search my memory, but I don't come up with anything.

That gets me thinking about how long it's been since

Dad died. I count the months on my fingers under the table.

Twenty-two and a half.

Almost twenty-three.

A long time. And no time at all.

"Why don't you ever go out?" Grace asks me.

"I don't know," I say.

"He's like a Cirque du Soleil performer," Reach says. "He prefers to be alone in the air."

"I've got a leotard on instead of underwear," I say to Reach. "Should I take off my pants and show you?"

"I'm allergic to sausage," Reach says.

The techies laugh.

"I think we should get him out more," Grace says.

"That we should," Reach says with a nod.

He spins the pizza tray so an available slice comes up in front of her.

"You want a slice, Grace?"

"I can throw in a couple bucks," she says.

"Don't worry about it. I've got you covered," Reach says.

Grace takes the slice.

"Is this your kinder, gentler side?" I say to Reach.

"Don't get used to it," he says.

"Check it out. We've got company," Benno says.

He points towards the front door where the actors are entering in a big group. Summer is with them.

Reach says, "Check your ammo, gentlemen."

Conversation dwindles to nothing as the actors pass by.

There's an uncomfortable moment when it seems like nobody is going to say anything. We're going to pretend we don't know each other.

Then Johanna breaks the ice.

"How's it going, techies?" she says.

"I prefer the term *stagehands*," Benno says. He twirls a mutton chop and stares at her boobs.

"Don't even talk to her," Reach says.

"Screw you, Reach," she says. "I'm trying to be decent."

Reach glares at her. While it's true we don't get along with actors, Reach and Johanna are mortal enemies. I've never understood why.

I look at Summer. I don't want her to see me hating actors with the rest of the techies. I smile so I seem a little different than everyone else.

"Are you laughing at us?" Jazmin says to me.

"I wasn't laughing," I say.

She looks at the pizza in front of me.

"You know cheese is bad for acne," she says. "All that oil."

I cover my face, embarrassed.

"At least we're buying the pizza and not serving it," Reach says. "Like you'll be doing after you graduate."

"I'll be acting," Jazmin says. "On Broadway."

"Right. There are, like, three roles and three million actors," Reach says.

"If we're not working, you're not working," Johanna says.

"That's why God made puppets and animatronics," Reach says. "Because he loves techies and wants us to work, even if you're not."

Wesley snorts. "Let's not waste our time," he says, and he puts his arms around Johanna's shoulders.

"I can walk by myself," she says, and she shrugs him off and stamps away.

"You'd better go tame your shrew," Reach says to Wesley, "and leave us to enjoy our dinner."

Wesley flips him the finger, then runs after Johanna. The rest of the actors follow. I try to make eye contact with Summer, but she's carried away by the group.

"You were a little hard on them, weren't you?" I say to Reach when they're gone.

"Seriously, Reach," Grace says, "why do you hate actors so much?"

"I don't hate them," Reach says. "They're an annoyance. Like jock itch. With good diction."

Grace laughs.

"Besides, they think they're better than us," Reach says.

"We think we're better than them," Half Crack says.

"But we are. They're delusional," Reach says.

While the techies argue with each other, I lean back, glancing across the room at the actors' table. Summer is in the middle of the group looking a little uncomfortable.

Grace leans over and whispers to me.

"Why don't you speak to her?"

"Speak to who?" I say.

"Come on. I see you staring," she says. "Talk to her and get it over with."

"I don't know how to talk to women," I say.

"News flash: you're talking to me."

"But you're a techie."

"I'm a *female* techie. Remember these babies?"

Grace sticks out her chest.

"Remember them? I almost lost an eye," I say.

Reach notices Grace's chest, gives it a quick once-over, then goes back to talking with the techies.

Grace says, "This whole story about not being able to talk to girls? Old news."

I look back at Summer. She's sitting in a booth with actors all around her.

I try to come up with some excuse for walking over to the table and pulling her away. What would I say? I think of different plays I've seen, the way men talk to women in those plays. But I can't imagine myself saying any of those things.

I stand up.

"I'm going to the bathroom," I say.

Grace looks disappointed.

I address the table in a fake Shakespearean accent.

"Gentlemen, I will away in haste to the can."

That's a techie tradition. All matters pertaining to the bathroom should be discussed loudly and often.

"Get thee to a lavatory!" Benno says.

"Give the toilet my regards," Reach says. "The way this pepperoni is hitting my gut, we're going to be spending quality time together in the near future."

For an Indian kid, Reach has no stomach for spicy foods. It's an embarrassment to his family. And it makes being in a stall next to him a less-than-attractive proposition.

"I've got toilet paper in my backpack if anyone needs," Half Crack says.

"Who carries their own TP?" Reach says.

"I love three-ply. Don't give me a hard time about it," Half Crack says.

"Okay, guys. I got to get this done," I say, and I head off.

I stop midway across the restaurant. There's no way to get to the bathroom without passing by the actors' table.

I glance back to the techies. Reach is preoccupied, showing some new iPhone app to Half Crack. Grace is looking over his shoulder.

I look back to the actor's table, and Summer looks up, noticing me.

That's when I have a brainstorm.

I take out my phone and pretend I'm getting a call. It's a great distraction when you're uncomfortable. You can hold the phone to your ear and wave to people, and everyone thinks you're busy.

I press the phone hard to my ear. I pretend I'm talking to Josh.

"Hey, bro!" I say to the dead phone. "Great to hear from you again!"

I keep talking while I walk quickly towards the bathroom.

"What's up at Cornell?" I say to the phone. "I hear that place is party central."

I rush past the actors' table.

"Where's the fire?" Wesley says.

"In his pants," Peter says.

I ignore them, running down the hall and slamming the restroom door behind me.

SHE HATH BLESSED AND ATTRACTIVE EYES.

I check my face in the mirror. I've been putting benzoyl peroxide on these zits for two days, but they've only gotten bigger. I wish I had some stage makeup to cover up the redness, but I left the tube of greasepaint in my backpack.

I spend a minute psyching myself up enough to walk by the actors' table again. I take a deep breath, open the door, and run right into Summer coming down the hall.

She points at me. "Z. That's your name."

"How did you find out?" I say.

"The actors told me."

She takes a step towards me, and I see her up close for the first time. I was right about her eyes. They're hazel with specks of other colors mixed in.

"You're staring," she says.

"Your eyes."

"Is something wrong with them?"

146

"They're a lot of different colors."

"That's because I'm a mutt," she says. "Our family tree looks like a Lonely Planet guide."

"Ours looks like a touring company of *Fiddler on the Roof*."

She laughs, a high-pitched sound like a birdcall.

"Was that a laugh?" I say.

"It's weird, isn't it?"

"More like distinctive."

"That's a nice way to put it," she says.

I look at the sign on the restroom. A figure of a man standing next to a woman, a wall between them.

There are so many things I want to say to Summer, but now that she's in front of me, I can't think of any of them.

She says, "Why did you lie to me, Z? You said you weren't in the hall when I was dancing, but you were."

"I was."

"And you were on spot after rehearsal the other night. You helped me with my monologue."

"Guilty."

"So what's the deal? Are you stalking me or something?"

"Definitely not stalking. It's not like I'm sending you my hair in an Altoids tin."

"Gross."

"You obviously don't know the techies," I say.

"So you're not a stalker. Why all the weirdness?"

"I don't mean to be weird. I'm just nervous."

"Around girls?"

"Around oxygen."

She laughs.

"And girls, too," I say.

I raise my hand to my zits, trying to cover them up without being too obvious.

"I get nervous, too," she says.

"What makes you nervous?"

"Getting a lead three days before opening night."

"That's pretty scary," I say.

"First I thought I wasn't good enough to get the role, now I think I'm not good enough to do it. Hysterical, right?"

"I think you're good enough."

"That's a nice thing to say. Even if you are lying."

"I'm not lying. I saw your monologue. It was great."

She bites at her lower lip.

"And now that I'm on spot, I can help you," I say.

"How can you help?"

"Light is pretty amazing."

"Will it memorize my lines for me?"

"If you ask it nicely."

She laughs. "Okay. What about the lighting guy?"

"What about him?"

"Would he run lines with me?"

"Are you serious?" I say.

"It's a terrible idea, isn't it? You must have a lot of tech stuff to do."

There's a loud laugh from the actors' table. Their voices carry down the hall towards us. "It's not that. I mean, why aren't you working with Johanna?"

"She kind of wants me dead right now. I replaced her best friend, remember?"

"I'd like to help," I say, "but there's the actors-versus-techies thing . . ."

"The code," she says.

"The code."

"Do you always follow the rules?"

I think about Grace and me in Derek's car.

"Not always," I say.

"Could you break a rule for me?"

"Maybe I could bend one. For the show."

She holds out her hand and we shake. Her hand is soft and warm, much warmer than I thought it would be.

"Can we meet tonight?" she says.

"Tonight is okay."

"Is it all right if I come to your place? My parents are mildly psychotic."

"Really? My mom is completely normal. At least since the lobotomy."

Summer laughs. "So what do you say?"

I think about how excited Mom would be if I had a girl over to the house. Too excited.

Then I remember she's going to be home late because of a work event.

"You can come over," I say.

Summer pulls out her cell phone.

"Type in your number, okay? I'll grab a bite with the actors, then I'll run home, change, and call you."

I put my number in her phone and hand it back.

"You're saving my life," Summer says. She steps forward and gives me a quick hug. She has this delicious fruit smell that makes me want to bury my face in her hair.

Reach comes walking around the corner, but he's looking back towards the actors.

"Talk to you later," I say, and I quickly turn away as she goes into the bathroom.

"What's up?" I say to Reach.

"Everything okay back here?" he says.

"I was just abusing the facilities."

"That's why I brought my oxygen mask," Reach says. He sighs, looks at me. "It's good to have you out with us."

"Interesting stuff happens when you come down from the catwalk."

"That's what I've been trying to tell you," Reach says. He sniffs the air. "Why does it smell like fruit back here?"

He wrinkles his nose and heads into the bathroom.

THIS IS THE WOMAN, BUT NOT THIS THE MAN.

"O weary night," Summer says, *"O long and tedious night."*

We're sitting in my living room running lines, practicing Summer's part over and over again until it's memorized.

It's exciting to be so close to Summer while she's acting. I've seen her from the wings, from the catwalk, even from the audience, but to have her three feet in front of me is amazing.

"Shine comforts from the east," Summer says. *"That I may back to Athens by daylight, from these that my poor company detest . . ."*

She tries to remember the next line but can't. She gets frustrated and punches herself in the thigh.

"Line," she says.

"And sleep," I say, reading from the script on my lap.

"That's right," she says. *"And sleep, that sometimes shuts up sorrow's eye . . ."*

"*Steal me awhile . . . ,*" I prompt.

"This is never going to work," she says. "I need to have this all memorized and I don't."

"Just try it again," I say. "*Steal me awhile . . .*"

"*Steal me awhile from mine own company,*" she says. "This is driving me crazy. It's hard to memorize something when you don't understand it."

"What don't you understand? Maybe we can figure it out together."

"Okay, for instance, 'Steal me awhile.' What does that mean?"

"I think it's like . . . Have you ever been so upset that you just want to sleep?"

"Like when things suck and all you want to do is escape."

"Like that," I say.

"*Steal me awhile from mine own company.* Turn off my brain for ten seconds."

"Right."

"Okay, check this out," she says.

She flings herself down on the sofa.

"What if I lay down after that line, but I keep my eyes open like I can't fall asleep. All I want to do is stop thinking, but I can't."

"Welcome to my life," I say.

She laughs.

"I'll go you one better," I say. "We could hold the light cue for a couple seconds, like the play can't continue until Helena sleeps, but she can't sleep."

"Can you do that?"

"If I were the lighting designer, I could. But that's Derek's territory."

"You could ask him," she says.

"No, I couldn't."

She sits up on the couch.

"Why not? He seems nice enough," she says.

"I think that depends," I say.

"On what?"

"On whether you have breasts."

"A lion among ladies, is a most dreadful thing," she says, quoting from the play.

"Are you talking about Derek?"

"More like a cat than a lion. But you get the idea," she says.

"I'm surprised."

"Girls aren't stupid, you know. We see what's going on."

"But a lot of girls go out with him."

"He's good looking," she says, like that explains everything.

"So if you're good looking, you can be a jerk?"

"It's not *just* that he's good looking. He's also a player. Which makes it kind of a challenge. You always think you're the special one, you know, the one who is going to make someone change."

"I never thought of that," I say.

"It explains a lot of things. Girls who date jerks. Girls who go out with gay guys. You know all the types."

"What type are you?"

She looks away, picks at some rough skin on her knee.

"That's kind of personal, Ziggy."

"What did you call me?"

"I don't know. Ziggy? It just popped out."

"Maybe it should pop back in."

"Do you hate it?" she says.

"Not hate," I say.

"That's the thing about pet names. You can't make them up. They have to occur spontaneously."

I feel sweat pooling under my arms. I stand up and head for the thermostat.

"I'm going to turn on some AC," I say.

"You can make up a pet name for me if it makes you feel better," Summer calls after me.

"It's kind of hard to make up a pet name for someone named Summer. I mean, the name is already perfect."

"You think I'm perfect?" she says, teasing me. "I thought you had issues with my name."

Before I can say anything, my phone starts to play "Jai Ho," the song from *Slumdog Millionaire*.

I press Ignore.

"You like Indian music?" Summer says.

"It's Reach," I say. "I got a new phone a few months ago, and he demanded creative control of his ringtone."

A shot of guilt goes through me. Reach hates when I press Ignore. And if he knew I ignored him because I had an actress over—

"I could use a break anyway," Summer says. "My head is about to explode."

"You want a soda?" I say as I head into the kitchen.

"Sure," she says. "You have diet?"

I open the refrigerator and let the cold air blow over me. I'm sweating like a pig, scared to say the wrong thing, scared to say nothing at all. I grab two cans of Diet Pepsi and head back into the living room.

Summer is standing on the other side of the room looking at one of Dad's paintings. It's an abstract, three long panels with gaps between them, the color jumping across the gaps and continuing, like water falling off the side of a cliff.

"This is amazing," she says.

"Yeah," I say.

I crack open a soda, sip from it.

Summer leans into the corner of the painting, looking at the name there.

"Ziegler," she says. "Did you paint this?"

"It was my dad."

"That's pretty cool to have a dad who's an artist. My dad is a CPA."

"He's gone," I say.

"Where did he go?" she says.

I study the Diet Pepsi can, look at the different shades of blue across the logo.

"He died," I say.

"I'm so sorry. When did it happen?"

"Two years ago. A little less than two."

She comes over and I hold out her soda. She takes it, but she doesn't move away. "That's not so long," she says.

"Sometimes it feels like a long time. Sometimes like no time at all."

"My dad's gone, too," she says. "Not like yours. I don't mean to compare us at all. I can't imagine what you—"

She stops herself.

"I sound like a jerk," she says.

"It's hard to talk about," I say. "That's why I usually don't."

"We can drop it," she says.

"No. Tell me about your dad."

"I just meant my dad's there, but he's gone. Like you call his name, and he doesn't answer even though he's sitting three feet away from you."

"Like a ghost dad," I say.

"Yeah, or Frankendad. From a horror movie or

something. I love watching horror movies; I just don't want my life to be one."

"I like Broadway musicals," I say.

"Really?"

"That sounds kind of gay, doesn't it?"

"Well . . . ," Summer says. "Are you gay?"

"No."

"So why does it have to be gay or straight? Can't it just be, I don't know, theater-iffic?"

"Theater-iffic?"

"It was the joke in my old school. We used 'theater' to describe everything. So stuff was theater-licious, theater-iffic, theater-ificent."

"Or the opposite. Drama-trocious," I say.

"Exactly!" she says.

"You have a nice smile," I say.

She closes her mouth fast.

"I don't like it," she says.

"Why not?"

She leans in until her face is about a foot away.

"Look," she says, and bites her lower lip with her teeth like a rabbit.

"You're doing a Bugs Bunny impression?"

"My tooth."

She points to her right tooth. There's a little yellow line that runs diagonally across it.

"What is that?" I say.

"I had an accident when I was a kid. I fell and broke my tooth, and they had to glue it back on."

"It doesn't look bad," I say.

"It's just one of those things," she says. "I think about it."

"I think about my acne."

"You have acne?"

"Very funny," I say.

"I know you have it," she says, "but I don't see it."

"What do you see?"

She studies my face for a second.

"I see you," she says.

I hear the sound of keys in the front door. Mom calls out, "I'm home, sweetie pie!"

"Sweetie pie, huh?" Summer says.

"Oh, God." I put my head in my hands.

Summer grins. "It looks like all the ladies in your life have pet names for you."

Mom walks into the room.

"Oh," Mom says. "You have company."

She freezes, not knowing what to do.

"Not company," I say. "Theater business. We're working on a show."

"Are you going to introduce us?" Mom says.

Summer extends a hand. "Hi, I'm Summer," she says.

"I'm Adam's mother. I apologize for being so surprised. Adam doesn't usually have girls over."

"Mom!" I say.

"It's true," Mom says.

"But you don't have to say it. Keep the mystery alive."

"You're so beautiful," Summer says to my mom.

Mom fights to get a loose piece of hair behind her ear.

"I'm a mess," she says. "I just got out of work."

"It doesn't matter. You have great bone structure," Summer says.

Mom laughs. "We're keeping this girl around," she says.

"It's nice meeting you," Summer says. "But it's getting late."

"Do you need a lift home?" Mom says.

"I can walk," Summer says.

"Nonsense," Mom says. "Why don't I give you a ride?"

"It's probably faster if she walks," I say.

Mom gives me a dirty look.

"She's not known for her driving prowess," I say to Summer.

"I wouldn't mind a ride," Summer says. "If it's not too much trouble."

"No trouble at all," Mom says, and they walk to the door, chatting like old friends.

I'm left standing in the living room, wondering what happened.

Mom says, "Are you coming, Adam?"

"Of course," I say, and I follow them.

"It's like he's in a trance," Mom says.

"He's drunk on Shakespeare," Summer says.

Mom says, "I don't think it's Shakespeare. I think it's—"

"Mystery, Mom!" I say.

"All right, all right," she says.

She and Summer giggle.

LET ME QUIET GO.

Summer and I sit in the back of Mom's car as she drives through the streets of Montclair. Mom is such a slow driver, it's hard to tell if she's going forward or backward.

"Take a left at the corner," Summer says.

Mom stops at the stop sign and then waits almost twenty seconds before taking the turn.

"We should have you home by morning," I whisper to Summer.

"Is everyone in your family so careful?" she says.

"There's a whole story behind it."

A Dad story, but I don't want to talk about that.

"Will you tell me sometime?" Summer says.

I nod.

Headlights pass by, briefly lighting up the inside of the car. I see Summer's face in profile looking out the window. It's like a snapshot, a second of Summer followed by blackness.

It makes me think about another time I was in the back of the car. A time with Josh.

We were in the backseat arguing about something. Mom turned around to tell us to cut it out. Only she wasn't driving. She was in the passenger seat.

It seems like such a small moment, barely worth a memory.

When was it?

I looked out the car window. Flowers bloomed on the side of the road, the hills sprinkled like a Monet painting.

When was it?

Now I remember.

It was summertime. Our last trip to New Hampshire.

Dad was driving.

"It's the yellow house on the right," Summer says.

She slides all the way over on the seat until she's pressed up against me.

"Thanks for your help," she whispers.

She gives me a kiss on the cheek.

It happens so quickly, I don't have time to react.

I wish I could freeze the moment. I'd like to stay here forever, next to Summer in the back of the car, her warm lips pressed to my face.

But it's over in a split second.

She slides back to her side of the car as Mom creeps to a stop in front of the yellow house.

"This is it," Summer says.

"I hope we see you again soon, Summer," my mom says.

"Me, too," Summer says. "See you at rehearsal, Ziggy."

She gets out and shuts the door.

Mom and I wait as she walks towards the house.

"Who's Ziggy?" Mom says.

"Forget it."

"But I'm interested."

"Mom!"

"Sorry," she says.

Summer disappears into her house. Mom puts the car in drive.

"Do you want to stay in the back?" she says.

"If it's okay. I like it back here."

There's something nice about riding in the back of a car. It makes you feel like a kid again.

Mom pulls away.

She doesn't say anything for two blocks, and then she says: "Is that the girl you were asking me about the other day?"

"Maybe."

"Are you two dating?"

"This is not the type of thing you want to discuss with your mother," I say.

"I'm sorry," Mom says.

"Stop saying sorry. You're driving me crazy."

I hear Mom sniffle.

The engine is whirring softly. Stars are twinkling.

Mom sniffles again.

"I'm sorry I'm the only one here for you to talk to," she says.

Suddenly the night feels heavy. It's all around the car, pressing in on me. It's hard to breathe. I get the empty feeling inside like I do in the dream.

I reach into the back pocket of the car seat and take out one of the glow sticks I store there. I crack it open and shake hard. The back of the car fills with a green glow.

Mom glances in the rearview mirror. She doesn't say anything. She's seen me do this before.

I hear a final long sniffle, and Mom blows her nose in a tissue.

"I'm sorry I yelled at you," I say.

Mom clears her throat.

"I don't want you to get upset," she says. "You've had enough of that. I want you to be happy."

"I know you do."

"If this girl could make you happy—"

"It's complicated, Mom. I can't explain."

"You could try."

"She's an actor," I say.

"Is that bad?"

"It's just . . . impossible."

"It sounds like a high-school thing."

"It is."

"Maybe you could call Josh and talk to him about it."

"Great idea," I say.

"He's good with these kinds of problems, isn't he?"

"Very good," I say. "I promise I'll call him."

"That makes me feel a lot better," Mom says.

I don't tell Mom I've called Josh half a dozen times in the last few months and he never calls me back.

She's stopped crying for now. That's all that matters.

YOU WOULD NOT MAKE ME SUCH AN ARGUMENT.

I'm picking up a replacement lamp from the Cave the next day when I hear Summer's voice.

"You can't pretend not to know me anymore," she says.

She's standing in the doorway in her costume. Not the fairy costume but Helena's costume, a short skirt with a black tank top. Summer is taller than Miranda, which makes her legs seem longer beneath the skirt.

She pokes her head through the door.

"Is this the secret lair?" she says.

"I wouldn't cross that threshold if I were you."

"What's going to happen?"

She lifts a foot and holds it in the air like she's going to step inside the Cave.

"We've never had an actor in here before. . . . Wait a minute. We did have one."

"You did?" she says.

"He's buried in the floor over there."

"You're funny, Ziggy."

She steps into the Cave.

"I'm not kidding. You shouldn't be in here."

She walks up to me and pinches my arm.

"It's exciting to break the rules, isn't it?" she says.

"Bend," I say. "Remember?"

"Right, right," she says. "By the way, I think your mom is cool."

"Are you sure you're talking about *my* mom?"

"Did she interrogate you on the way home?"

"A little water boarding. You know. The usual."

"She cares about you. That's more than I can say about my parents."

"Your parents don't care?" I say.

"They care. It's just that they're sort of . . . self-involved."

"I know what you mean."

She says, "I was thinking about a lot of stuff after you dropped me off last night."

I take a deep breath. I was thinking about a lot of stuff, too.

Romantic stuff.

Is it possible she was feeling the same way? Maybe this is my Josh moment. Summer is going to get nervous, twirl her hair, and declare her love.

"What were you thinking?" I say, getting ready for the big moment.

"What if I work and work for the next two days—and I'm still no good?" Summer says.

I look away from her. I stare at the pictures on the Wall of Fame.

"What if I don't have what it takes to be an actor, Ziggy? And I've been kidding myself all these years."

I feel like an idiot. I'm thinking about romance, and she's thinking about her acting career.

Techies and actors. Maybe we're supposed to be separate. Maybe it's better that way.

Maybe Reach is right.

"Do you think that's possible?" Summer says.

I still can't look at her.

"You've got nothing to worry about," I say. "You're going to be great."

Summer puts her hand on my upper arm. I turn towards her. Her eyes look green in the darkness of the Cave.

"Do you know what I like about you?" she says. "You totally get me. It's pretty rare that someone gets you so well."

"I get him," Reach says.

His voice is loud in the empty room. He's standing in the door of the Cave, his face tight and angry.

"I also get that we're starting tech in five minutes and

Mr. Ziegler has work to do. Real, non-acting work. The kind that gets your hands dirty."

"Sorry," Summer says. She rolls her eyes at me. "Talk to you later, Ziggy."

Reach steps aside so she can go out, then blocks the door behind her.

"Who the hell is Ziggy?" he says.

"That's what she calls me."

"Pet names? Son of a bitch. You've crossed over to the dark side and I had no idea."

He storms into the room, flipping the black curtain hard across the doorway behind him.

"You promised you'd tell me everything," he says. "So let's hear it."

"There's nothing to tell," I say.

"You said there was a woman. You said she was in the theater."

"I also said she didn't go to this school."

"Two truths, one lie. I know that game."

"There's only one truth," I say. "She's interesting, but she's an actor. End of story."

"Okay. This is where the malfunction is occurring. We do not find actors interesting, because they are not interesting. They are boring. They are good to look at, yes. I cannot deny that. They have been genetically selected to be good looking. Like a butterfly. A butterfly is a lovely thing, but when it comes time for brain surgery, you do not want a butterfly scrubbing in. You want a *doctor*. You want skill set."

"What are you talking about, Reach?"

"It's the same with a girlfriend."

"You want a girlfriend who's good with a scalpel?" I say.

"No. You want a girl with a brain. And there's nothing wrong with looks. But not an actor. For God's sake. I can't believe you would screw us up like that."

"How could that screw us up?"

"You'll start a war with the actors."

"We're already at war," I say.

"Right, but it's a cold war. There's a difference," Reach says.

"What about you?" I say. "You bought Grace a slice."

Reach's face turns red.

"That's different," he says.

"How is it different? You said she was on our Do Not Call List."

"She's a fallen techie, not an actor. It's a different rule."

"That's the problem with the rules. They're *your* rules. You can change them whenever you want."

"Places, please," Ignacio calls as he passes by the door. "Places!"

That's our cue to get into position.

"Drop it with this actor," Reach says. "Before it gets out of hand."

The lights flicker, signaling the run-through is about to begin.

Reach looks into my eyes.

"Promise me," he says. "For all our sakes."

"I promise."

I think about the pact Reach and I made when we were ten. No secrets, no matter what.

We've had our ups and downs over the years. I've avoided him, changed the subject, made fun of him, even argued with him.

But I never lied to his face. Not until now.

SEEKING SWEET FAVOURS.

I step out of the Cave and Derek gives me the *come here* gesture with his finger.

The finger gesture makes most people seem like a-holes, but when Derek does it, he makes you feel like you're lucky to be beckoned.

"I'm kind of in a rush," I say. "Ignacio called places."

"There are no places without me," Derek says. "I *am* places."

He relaxes against the wall while techies and actors rush past.

"I know the show is still rough, but I want you to know you've exceeded my expectations on spot."

"Thanks," I say.

He looks up and down the hall to make sure we're alone.

"Can I confide something to you? I've got one more year here, and I want it to be the biggest year ever. A drama in the fall, a musical in the winter, a comedy in the spring. Who knows, maybe I'll direct."

"What about Mr. Apple?" I say.

"He's a lame duck. I can go over his head if I have to. I've got pull."

"What kind of pull?" I say.

"Major pull. You know about my father, right?"

"I've heard of him."

More than heard of him. Thomas Dunkirk. He's the kind of guy who can call up the head of Lincoln Center and ask for a favor. *Hey, I'm designing your new building. Did I mention my son is interested in theater?*

"He's coming to see the show," Derek says.

"That's great," I say.

"I want to show him what I can do. What we all can do. This may not be LaGuardia Arts, but that's no reflection on our talent. Do you know what I mean?"

"Absolutely."

"So everything has to be perfect," Derek says.

Summer walks by in costume, her pale thighs peeking out from under her skirt. Derek glances at her, then looks back at me.

"I want to be the first student to design and direct on the big stage. Everything. Start to finish. The theatrical equivalent of Quentin Tarantino. Write, produce, shoot, edit."

"Impressive. If you can pull it off," I say.

"I can pull it off. Have no doubt. But I need technical know-how behind me. I need a strong board op. Someone who can lead the crew in this area."

"What about Benno?"

"Mutton Chops? Forget about him. We're talking about you."

I imagine being up in the booth, the computer board in front of me, watching dozens of lights go on and off as I press a button. I have to admit it's exciting. There's just one problem. The techie code is very clear about something like this.

You don't betray a fellow techie.

But is it a betrayal if Derek decides to take the board away from Benno and give it to me? Maybe that's just a promotion.

"You help me do what I want to do," Derek says, "and next year you write your own ticket. You want to design lights? Design a whole production? I'll back you."

Derek stares at me, trying to gauge my reaction.

"I got your attention, didn't I?" he says.

"You did."

"I thought so." Derek puts a hand on my shoulder, just like my father used to do.

I wonder if I was wrong about Derek. Maybe he's looking out for me, for all of us. Sure, he's ambitious, but that's another way of saying he has vision. He's an artist, like Dad was. And he wants to go places.

Maybe we can go places together.

He gives my shoulder a squeeze. "By the way, I saw you chatting with the new actor. You two aren't—"

He makes a *together* gesture with his fingers.

"Not exactly," I say.

"Let me be more precise," he says. "Have you gone out with her?"

"No."

"Have you even asked her out?"

"Not technically, no."

"Then *technically* it's every man for himself."

"I guess so. Yes."

"Good man," he says. He throws me a two-fingered salute then heads out to the tech table.

I'm so stunned, it takes me a minute to realize what just happened.

I want to run after Derek and start the conversation all over again. When he asks me about Summer, I'll lie and say, "She's my girlfriend. We've been going out for a month. Stay away from her."

I'll say, "You've already been with every girl in the theater department. You can't have her."

I'll say, "If you go near her, my brother Josh will kick your ass."

But I don't do any of that. I do what I always do.

I climb.

TRAGICAL,
MY NOBLE LORD, IT IS.

From the catwalk, I watch as rehearsal goes from bad to worse. It's like seeing a train derail in slow motion. You know something awful is happening, but you're powerless to do anything but watch. And if it looks terrible from up here, I can only imagine what it looks like from a theater seat.

Well, I don't have to imagine. Mr. Apple is making it pretty obvious.

"Goddam it," he says under his breath over and over again. He's been huffing and sighing all rehearsal, growing more and more angry in the dark.

At the beginning of Act II, Summer is straddling a tree stump that is supposed to swing out from behind her when she sits. But when she tries, it doesn't budge.

"It won't move," she says.

"Goddam it," Mr. Apple says again down below.

Grace jumps out onstage wearing a tool belt.

"I'll get it," she says.

Derek is up in the audience and running.

"Don't touch that," he says.

"It's no problem," Grace says, taking a set of pliers from her belt.

"Stop!" Derek shouts.

He leaps from the pit onto the stage where Summer is sitting.

"There's been enough human error tonight," he says. "Let a professional take over."

Grace looks like she's about to tear him a new one. But instead she steps back, smiles, and holds the pliers out to Derek.

"All yours, Double D," she says.

Derek scowls and snatches the pliers out of her hands.

"This will be a quick fix," he says.

He gives Mr. Apple a thumbs-up then bends over behind Summer.

She starts to get up.

"No, stay there," Derek says. "I promise this won't hurt a bit."

He fiddles with something around her butt.

"What are you adjusting exactly?" Summer says.

The actors laugh.

"True that it's difficult to adjust perfection," he says.

I'm praying he won't be able to fix the problem, that he'll look like an idiot in front of everyone.

But he twists his wrist for a couple seconds, then steps back.

The stump swings freely on its hinge now. There's a spattering of applause.

"And Bob's your uncle," Derek says.

He tosses the pliers in the air and catches them one-handed before passing them back to Grace.

"How lovely," Mr. Apple says. "That should cinch you the Tony for Best Stump this season. Now *continue*!"

                          WESLEY

          I do not, nor I cannot love you?

                          SUMMER

          And even for that do I love you the more.

The stump breaks and Summer tumbles to the floor. Wesley jumps forward to catch her and trips over her instead, which sends him flying into Peter, who bangs into Johanna. All four of them go down like dominoes.

"Stop!" Mr. Apple shouts. "Stop! *Stop!*"

Carol Channing leaps off Mr. Apple's lap and spins in a circle, yelping.

"My God," Mr. Apple says. "This is terrible."

He buries his face in his hands.

"I was about to say my line," Wesley says from the floor.

"It gets worse when you speak," Mr. Apple says.

"That's not cool—" Wesley says.

"We're trying to act," Johanna says, "but someone keeps pausing because they don't know their lines."

She indicates Summer.

"I'm doing my best, too," Summer says.

"Maybe your best isn't good enough," Johanna says.

Summer looks up, desperation in her eyes. I wish I could signal her somehow, tell her she's doing okay, but I know she can't see me behind the light.

"Take it easy," Peter says. "She's had the role for a day and a half."

"She could have it for a year and a half and it wouldn't matter," Johanna says.

The actors split into warring group, arguments breaking out all over the stage.

"Excuse me," Mr. Apple says.

He's ignored.

"Hello?" he says.

Wesley pushes Peter and he bumps into a set piece. Now Derek is up and shouting at the actors. Everyone is yelling at everyone else. Total chaos.

"I hate my life," Mr. Apple says quietly beneath me. He puts his head in his hands.

Derek is gesticulating wildly onstage, trying to show the actors where they should walk to avoid trouble. Meanwhile the headset is filled with chatter, techies blaming one another for various mistakes.

"I—HATE—MY—LIFE!!!" Mr. Apple bellows at the top of his lungs.

The theater goes silent. Everyone freezes.

"I hate my life, I hate this theater, I hate Shakespeare. *I hate salmon croquettes!*"

He throws his script on the ground.

"He's freaking out," Peter says.

"You know what else I hate?" Mr. Apple says. "I hate Sylvester for making me pay half the rent. I'm an *artist*! I need a sugar daddy. Then I could spend my days doing yoga and getting pedicures like Tad. And I could do my little plays at night. Tad has a theater company, *and* he gets pedicures. Where is my pedicure? Where is my Kundalini?"

"Who's Tad?" Johanna says.

"I so don't want to be gay right now," Peter says, covering his face with his hands.

Mr. Apple rifles through his briefcase until he comes up with his brown paper bag. He paces up and down the aisle breathing into it.

"You're scaring us, Mr. Apple," Johanna says.

"What should we do?" Summer says.

"Seriously," Wesley says. "Tell us what we should do and we'll do it."

Mr. Apple puts down the bag.

"This is supposed to be a love story," he says. "Haven't any of you been in love?"

The actors look at each other.

"Sort of," Wesley says.

"That's not what you said last week," Johanna says.

"I can't be responsible for what I say during a make-out session."

Johanna punches him.

"I'm not talking about high-school love," Mr. Apple says. "I'm talking about the big L, passion, the kind of love they write plays about. The kind of love that makes you go to acting school when your mother wants you to be a dentist. The kind of love that has you marrying your boyfriend even though he's a social worker specializing in HIV prevention in underserved communities, and you have exactly zero chance of buying a condo."

Mr. Apple gets upset again and buries his face in the paper bag. He mumbles to himself as he paces the floor.

"Why is he talking about real estate?" Hubbard says.

"I think he's having a nervous breakdown," Peter says.

"I was this close to dental school," Mr. Apple says, measuring off an inch with his fingers. "I could taste the nitrous oxide. But I had passion. I had to move to the city to eat ramen noodles and go to Stella Adler. And what good did it do me? I end up at Montclair friggin' High School. My personal vision of hell. No more. No more!"

He *pops* the paper bag with his fist. Then he packs his briefcase, jamming sheets of paper into the bottom.

"I've had enough," Mr. Apple says.

There's a gasp from the actors.

Derek says, "Please, Mr. Apple. Let's step out and discuss this."

"There's nothing to discuss, Mr. Dunkirk. I'm out of inspiration, and none of you seems to have had any to begin with."

He flings his briefcase over his shoulder.

"Please, Mr. Apple," Derek says.

Derek steps towards him, but Mr. Apple holds up a hand to stop him.

"I refuse to be a part of bad high-school production number three thousand four hundred and infinity. Directed by Jonathan Apple Jr., fat failure."

He rushes up the aisle and throws open the theater door.

A white blur shoots up the center aisle and passes through the door with a loud *yelp*.

"Carol Channing! You screwed up my exit again," he says, and he chases her out.

Nobody speaks for a long time.

"That was horrible," Johanna says.

"I've never seen a teacher have a meltdown before," Peter says.

"That wasn't a meltdown. That was Chernobyl," Wesley says.

"What's Chernobyl?" Johanna says.

"What do we do now?" Summer says.

I watch as the actors fall apart onstage. Some of them cry, some stand around, shocked. I wait for Reach or a techie to make a crack on the headset—anything to take the edge off—but it's silent.

I climb down the ladder and join the crowd onstage.

It's the perfect time for an inspirational song, à la *Les Misérables*. I imagine myself standing in front of the actors, waving a flag, rallying them to the cause.

We have to fight, I say. *It can't end like this.*

And then I burst into song. It begins as a solo, but it swells into a group number with full chorus.

The problem is I don't know how to inspire people.

But Derek does. He walks to the front of the stage, then hoists himself up into the middle of the actors. His voice is soft, almost a whisper.

"I'm sorry you had to see that," he says. "I'm sorry *I* had to see it. Mr. Apple is clearly distraught and doesn't know what he's saying."

"We open in two days," Jazmin says.

"How can we open without a director?" Johanna says.

Derek thinks for a moment.

"Right you are," he says. "We need a director. . . ."

He scratches his chin.

"What are you thinking?" Wesley says.

I start to get a bad feeling. Derek is too excited by Mr. Apple walking out. I edge towards the side exit.

"Where are you going?" Reach whispers

"I have to find Mr. Apple," I say. "Fast."

I rush out the back of the theater.

I run through the halls of the theater department. I look for Mr. Apple around the rehearsal rooms. I check his office, but the door is locked.

I start to panic, thinking he may have already gone home.

I rush out to the school parking lot.

There are only a few cars left in the lot, and one of them is Mr. Apple's Civic. From across the parking lot, I can see him sitting inside, the seat pushed all the way back so his stomach doesn't hit the wheel. As I get closer, I notice he's chewing rapid fire, his hand moving from the seat to his mouth in a blur. A box of Hostess Cakes is torn open next to him, the plastic wrappers scattered across his lap. He looks up, startled to see me. There are tears coming down his eyes as he sticks a chocolate cake in his mouth.

"Mr. Apple," I say.

He peeks at me through an inch of open window. He wipes snot from his nose.

"Are you okay?" I say.

He starts the car.

"We need you," I say.

"You don't need me," he says. "You need someone who cares about you. Who cares about the theater. The way it's supposed to be."

"Please don't go," I say.

He wipes tears from his eyes.

"I'm sorry, lad."

He rolls up the window and backs out of the space, his tires squealing as he speeds from the parking lot.

I stand there stunned, watching him go.

I hear the voices of the techies behind me.

I turn to find the cast and crew streaming out the back door of the school.

"You're too late," I tell Reach. "He's already gone."

"We're not here for him," Reach says. "We're going on a field trip."

"What?"

"A journey to find love. That's what Derek called it."

"Where can we find love?"

"In the city."

"That's crazy," I say.

"No kidding. Love is expensive in the city. Have you read the back of *The Village Voice*?"

"Seriously. What's the plan?"

"There's a Shakespeare film festival in the Village. Derek wants us to get inspired, and the actors are backing him. Either we go along with the plan or . . ."

"Or what?"

"Or nothing. There's not really an option."

I think about the train ride to Manhattan, and I start to get afraid. I can barely remember the last time I was there. I only know it was with Dad.

"I haven't been to the city in a long time," I say.

Reach studies my face.

"We'll go together," he says. "Just stay close to me. And for God's sake, stop worrying so much."

I WILL GO WITH THEE.

Reach and I take the train to Penn Station along with the techies, then we catch the subway down to the Village. When we get to Film Forum, the actors are standing around outside.

"Twenty-eight times," Johanna says.

"Thirty-two times," Jazmin says. "Including six performances of *Wicked*, but that totally counts."

"No way. We said *productions*, not *performances*," Johanna says.

"What are you guys talking about?" Half Crack says.

Johanna looks at him like he just pooped on her shoe.

"We're comparing how many Broadway shows we've been to," Jazmin says. "How many *productions*."

"I've been to fourteen," Hubbard says.

"Why so few?" Johanna says.

"My dad doesn't like me to come to the city. He thinks I'll get molested," Hubbard says.

"By who? The Disney characters? The city is totally safe now," Reach says.

"What are you guys even doing here?" Jazmin says. "We wouldn't be in this mess if it weren't for you."

"You're saying it's our fault Apple freaked?" Benno says.

"You drove him to it," Wesley says.

"If you guys could act, we'd still be at the theater right now," Reach says, looking at Johanna.

"Don't talk to her," Wesley says.

"I'll talk to whoever I want to talk to," Reach says.

"He's right. Don't talk to me," Johanna says.

I feel Reach tense up next to me.

The actors push forward in a group, coming right up against the line of techies. It feels like we're going to have a *West Side Story*–style gang war.

Derek walks up wearing a sport coat and button-down shirt. Summer is with him, also dressed up. It almost looks like they came together.

It's every man for himself, Derek said to me.

Is it possible he's already made his move?

"Good evening, theater folk," Derek says.

He looks from the actors to the techies, a sea of angry faces.

"What happening here?" he says.

"The techies are talking crap about us," Johanna says.

"Not crap. Truth," Benno says.

"We're just blowing off steam," I say. "Everyone's upset."

"It's easy to assign blame at a time like this," Derek says. "But let's use that energy to make the show better."

"How is a field trip going to make the show better?" Reach says.

"A day may sink or save a realm," Derek says.

"Is that Tennyson?" Jazmin says.

"Right you are," Derek says.

"What does it mean?" Wesley says.

"It means be patient. I'm working behind the scenes. Give me a day, and we shall see."

He moves off towards the ticket window, the actors following.

"You think he can save the show?" I say.

"I'm not one to root for Saggy D," Reach says, "but in this case, I'm hoping he's not full of it."

He takes a clutch of singles out of his pocket.

"Let's see some cash, gentlemen. These tickets aren't going to buy themselves."

The techies go inside. I look towards the ticket window, where I see Derek pull Summer off to the side and whisper to her. She takes out her phone like she's getting a call, and he excuses himself and walks away.

Right away my phone buzzes. It's a text from Summer: *Hlp! Mdn n dstrss.*

I go into the theater. Summer is standing near the water fountain. I hold up my phone.

"What's *mdn n dstrss?*" I say.

"Maiden in distress."

"You're texting Shakespeare?"

"Pretty cool, huh?"

"Seriously cool. But what's the distress?"

"I'm trying to repel the British invasion."

She glances towards Derek.

"You didn't come together?" I say.

"Are you kidding? He saw me walking from the subway and attached himself to me."

A couple of techies are looking our way, so I lean down and take a drink, pretending I'm not talking to her.

"I've got an idea, Ziggy. Everyone is going to see *As You Like It*, and I don't like it. What if we try plan B?"

"What's plan B?"

She shifts her eyes towards theater two. Kurosawa's *Throne of Blood.*

"It's the Scottish play, Japanese-style. Way more interesting," she says.

"You want to blow everyone off?" I say.

Reach is walking towards the techies with tickets in his hand.

"We're not blowing them off. We'll be right next door," Summer says.

I look from Derek to Reach, thinking about all the potential trouble I could get into.

Summer leans over and drinks from the fountain. Cleavage appears in the V of her shirt collar. The cold water hits her lips.

I feel braver than I did a moment ago.

"Let's go to the Kurosawa," I say.

Summer gives me a satisfied nod.

"Now we need a distraction," she says.

"I could fall over and start foaming at the mouth."

"Techies do that all the time," she says with a wink. "I have a better idea."

She disappears into the crowd in the lobby, then pops out of the far hallway like she just came out of the women's room.

"Oh my God. I think I saw Kristin Chenoweth in the bathroom!" she says.

"Kristen Chenoweth? Are you kidding?" Johanna says.

"It's a total star sighting," Summer says.

"Miranda loves her. I wish she were here," Johanna says.

"*We're* here," Jazmin says.

She rushes towards the bathroom, the actors following behind.

"Don't stalk her," Peter says, rushing along behind them.

"What's going on?" Half Crack says.

"Some famous actress," I say.

"Is she hot?"

"Evidently," I say.

That's all it takes to send the techies stampeding towards the bathroom, too.

It comes down to Derek, Summer, and me, looking at each other in the lobby.

"You don't want to see her?" Summer asks him.

"I've seen my share of stars," Derek says. "Dad has dinner parties. You know how it is."

"I think she was with Kate Winslet," Summer says. "Aren't they doing *The Cherry Orchard* together?"

Derek's mouth drops open.

"Maybe I'll take a quick peek," he says, and heads towards the bathrooms.

Summer grabs my arm.

"Come on!" she says, pulling me into theater two.

I glance behind us at the lobby, now empty of students.

Almost empty.

Grace is standing by the refreshment stand, watching us go.

I DO QUAKE WITH FEAR.

"It's like we're on a secret mission," Summer says after we duck into the theater.

"I wish our secret mission had popcorn," I say.

"Me, too, but we can't go out there again."

She scans the theater.

"Where do you like to sit?" she says.

"Anywhere."

"Do you prefer front, middle, or back?"

"I prefer the ceiling."

She laughs. A few people turn around and look at us.

"That option is off the table for tonight," she says, "so I choose the middle."

We shuffle in and sit down. I squirm, looking all around.

"It's strange to be an audience member," I say.

"For me, too. Every time I go to the movies, I want to be on the screen."

"And I want to be behind the projector."

"We're freaks," Summer says.

"We're theater freaks," I say. "That's a little different than regular freaks."

"Much cooler," Summer says.

The lights go down, and the trailers start.

Summer leans over and whispers in my ear:

"We should be in rehearsal right now. Not watching a stupid movie." Panic creeps into her voice. "What if the show gets canceled? What if I never get to do the role?"

"It will be okay," I say. "I'm sure of it."

I'm not sure of anything, but I feel like I have to be strong for Summer. It's funny how that works. Sometimes being around a girl makes you act braver than you really are.

Summer sighs, and I feel her relax into the seat next to me.

The trailers end and *Throne of Blood* starts.

The first scene is a shot of an ancient castle enveloped in fog. Toshiro Mifune rides up out of the murk and shouts, "Open the gates!"

The title card flashes.

It begins.

Throne of Blood is based on the Scottish play, the one we don't say out loud because it's bad luck. In Kurosawa's version, the Scottish king is a Japanese lord who goes power mad, plotting and scheming to find a way to become Emperor. It's a story about ambition driving people crazy.

A little like our theater department.

Summer shifts in her seat, and our elbows brush against each other in the dark. I take a deep breath, and my nose fills with her delicious scent.

"What are you wearing?" I whisper.

"You mean my underwear? That's a little personal, Ziggy."

"I meant your perfume."

"Good, because I'm not wearing underwear."

"Shhh," an audience member says.

"Just kidding," Summer whispers, and elbows me in the side.

We watch the movie for a minute, then she leans over again.

"I don't wear any perfume," she says.

"Your skin just naturally smells of apples?"

She grabs her hair. "That must be my shampoo. Is it bad?"

"It's great."

She smiles, her face lit by the glow of the screen.

"Ziggy? Do you like how I smell?"

"*Shhh!*" the audience member says, louder this time.

"Sorry," I say.

And I settle in to watch the film.

ALLEN ZADOFF

About twenty minutes into it, the image starts to shift on the screen.

"What's going on?" Summer says.

"Maybe it's a bad print," I say.

"Oh," Summer says.

After a second she says, "What's a bad print?"

"I have no idea. I was trying to sound like a techie."

She laughs, a loud *peep* that earns us another *shhhh* from behind.

A few minutes later there's a scraping sound from the projection booth, and the film jams. For a second we watch the tug-of-war of frame versus screen, followed by a grinding sound as the projector shuts down. The screen goes black.

A groan passes through the crowd. Someone shouts in Japanese, and a few people laugh. Someone else jumps up and goes to find an usher.

Meanwhile, we sit in the dark.

At first I'm okay. Then my chest starts to tighten and it gets tough to breathe. I can hear myself wheezing, but I feel far away, my mind and body separated by miles.

"Ziggy?"

"What?"

My voice comes out in a gasp.

"Are you okay?"

I try to answer but I can't.

My father is driving at night, his spotlight beams illuminating trees in the distance. I'm in the passenger seat next to him.

"What's going on?" Summer says.

My father switches from high beams to low, the light now shining on wet pavement. The tires squeal as he takes a corner. I gasp and check my seat belt.

"What should I do?" Summer says.

I try to get back to the theater. If I can hold on for another minute, the lights will come on and everything will be fine.

But it's dark now. Nothing feels fine when it's dark.

I feel something brush my hand. It's my father reaching across to me in the car. I yank my hand away fast. It's not that I don't want to hold my father's hand. But if I let him touch me, I'll have to feel him let go. That's the part I can't stand.

"It's me," Summer whispers.

I feel the touch again.

It's warm. Soft.

Summer's hand on mine.

I relax my arm, spread my fingers. Her hand slides into mine.

I look for my father in the car, but I see nothing.

The pitch-black of the theater.

I'm back.

"Are you sick, Adam?" she says.

I feel my chest relaxing.

ALLEN ZADOFF

"No. But don't let go, okay?" I say.

"I won't."

"Promise?"

She squeezes me tighter.

There's some noise from the projection booth, and the film starts up again. The audience applauds.

I breathe and watch the movie, my body slowly returning to normal.

After a minute I shift my arm a little, thinking now that the movie is on, Summer won't want to hold my hand anymore. But she hangs on.

We sit like that for what seems like a long time. Our hands start to sweat, or at least mine does. It's hard to know who is doing the sweating when your hands are sealed together.

I try to watch the movie, but I can't stop thinking how disgusting my hand must be.

Finally, I can't stand it anymore.

I take my hand away and wipe it on my pant leg.

Right away I wish I hadn't.

Summer shifts in her seat but she doesn't say anything.

I sit for the rest of the movie, wanting to take Summer's hand, wishing she would take mine, but neither of us doing anything about it.

LET US LISTEN TO THE MOON.

The other film still hasn't finished when we walk into the lobby.

I say, "Maybe we should sneak in the back. Then we can pretend we saw the whole thing."

"We're either caught or we're not caught," Summer says. "We might as well enjoy ourselves in the meantime."

"How do we do that?"

"We could take a walk."

I look out at the street through the Film Forum window.

"Don't worry, Ziggy. I'm not going to kidnap you."

"It's not that. I just haven't been to the city in a long time."

"Perfect," she says. "I know the Village a little bit. There's a great gelato place around the corner."

She takes my arm and pulls me out the front door.

It's past nine o'clock and the sun is down, but the city feels bright and awake. Montclair is a ghost town by this hour. But here the store windows are lit up and the streets are busy. I try to imagine living in place that's never dark. It seems like paradise.

Summer and I get gelato and walk down the street together. It's not full-on summer weather yet, but it's warm enough that people are out and moving up and down the sidewalk. Even though it's Wednesday night, the energy is exciting, like the beginning of the weekend. New York always feels like the weekend to me. Maybe it's because Dad and I came on the weekends. Or maybe the city is just like that.

I take a little spoonful of chocolate gelato and swirl it around in my mouth.

"What do you like about tech?" Summer says.

"Everything."

"But what about it? Specifically."

"The answer might bore you to death. Then I'll have to explain to the police why there's a body on the sidewalk."

"I'll tell you what. Start talking and if I'm bored, I'll send up a warning flare."

I think of all the reasons I love tech. The hard work. The feeling of being on a team with people you like. The way every situation is a riddle you have to solve, and you can't just solve it any old way, because in tech, the simplest solutions are usually the best. So you have to be kind of ingenious about it.

And then there's light.

I could talk about that for a week without running out of things to say.

"You're not going to tell me?" Summer says.

"I'm trying. There's so much. I don't know where to start."

"Tell me one thing," she says.

"Illusion," I say.

"What about it?"

"Think of a set. On the audience's side, everything looks real and finished, but on the other side it's raw—tape, screws, and wood."

"I know what you mean. You can stand backstage and see both things at the same time."

"We can, but the audience never does. To them it's this perfect illusion. Maybe not perfect, but they believe it, right? What do they call that?"

"Suspension of disbelief."

"Right. You know it's not real, but you want to believe it is."

"So you like fooling the audience?"

"Not fooling them," I say. "More like taking them to another place. They go because they want to. And because the techies made them believe it. We constructed it."

"What about the actors?"

"Right. You guys are there, too," I say.

"No wonder the actors hate you," she says, and she punches me in the arm.

"Why do you like acting?" I say.

"I always wanted to be an actress. Since I was six years old."

"What did you want to be before that?"

"The daughter of an actress."

I laugh.

"That's why the role is so important to me. I have to prove I'm an actor, Ziggy."

"But you are an actor."

"I'm an actor in my bedroom in front of the mirror. I want to be one in the real world."

"You don't have to prove it to me," I say. "I already know you're good."

"How do you know?"

"I just do."

"That's nice of you to say."

I look at Summer, her face crimson in the reflection of a cigar store sign. I get this crazy feeling that we're going to kiss. This is the moment.

I thought a kiss moment was a myth. I've seen them in the movies, but I've never felt one in real life before.

I feel it now.

There's a long pause, both of us looking at each other like we're waiting for something to happen—

Then a taxi honks. A foreign couple cuts between us, arguing in heavy accents about which subway to take.

The kiss moment passes.

Maybe it was never there at all. I can't be sure.

"We should get back," I say.

"Let's run away to the city," Summer says. "We'll live in the Village and do theater all day and night."

"But rent is, like, three thousand bucks a month here."

"Dream, meet cold water."

"Sorry."

"You never thought of living in the city?"

"I used to. Not anymore."

"What changed?"

"Everything."

She stares down at the sidewalk.

"You seem like a sad person," she says.

"I'm not sad."

"I think you are," she says. "Maybe you're so used to it, you don't notice."

We turn the corner and head south onto Sixth Avenue. There's a line of restaurants, each with a swarm of people outside, clinking glasses and laughing.

I keep thinking about what Summer said.

"I don't feel sad when I'm with you," I say.

"What do you feel?"

Before I can answer, we turn onto Houston Street. The actors and techies are standing in a big group in front of Film Forum.

"We found them," Ignacio says into his cell as soon as he sees us.

The crowd rushes towards us.

"You didn't answer your text. We thought you got kidnapped or something," Johanna says.

"We were taking a walk," Summer says.

The techies and actors split into groups, one centered around me and one around Summer.

"Where the hell did you go?" Reach says.

"We went to the Kurosawa film," I say.

Reach glares at the cup in my hand.

"And you got ice cream," Reach says.

"It's gelato."

"Son of a bitch! You know how I feel about gelato. It's arrogant ice cream."

I try to get Summer's attention, but I can't find her through the crowd.

"You dumped us for gelato," Reach says.

"It wasn't like that," I say.

Grace watches me, her face blank.

"I want to talk to you inside. Right now," Reach says.

He storms past Derek into the theater.

"Trouble in techie paradise?" Derek says.

"He thinks I blew him off," I say.

Derek puts his arm around my shoulders and walks me a few steps away.

"I know why he's upset," Derek says. "This was supposed to be a team-building exercise, and you ditched us. That's not cool at all."

"Sorry."

"I should be angry at you, but your little side excursion had an unintended consequence. You brought us together better than anything I could have planned."

"Glad I could help," I say with a little laugh.

But Derek doesn't laugh. He steps up to me, his face two inches from mine.

"Go in there and make it right," Derek says.

He points to Reach pacing back and forth inside the theater. I look at Summer outside on the sidewalk, surrounded by actors.

"Business before pleasure," Derek says. "Help me get everyone on the same page for tomorrow's rehearsal."

"What rehearsal? Mr. Apple quit."

"He did. But the show must go on."

I study Derek's face, looking for some clue as to what he's planning.

Summer interrupts us.

"This is all my fault, Derek," she says. "Don't be angry with him."

"Not your fault at all," Derek says. "And no one is angry."

Reach bangs on the window of the theater.

"Well, certain people are angry," Derek says. He gives me a knowing look.

"We're leaving now," Johanna says.

"Wait up. I'll walk you guys to the train," Derek says. "Business first," he says to me, and he joins the actors.

Summer and I look at each other.

"This is a mess," Summer says.

Reach bangs on the theater window again.

"Summer!" Wesley calls.

"It was worth it," I say to Summer.

I walk into the theater. Reach leaps on me.

"I can't believe you," he says. "You disappeared without telling anyone. In the city!"

"It's New York. Not Baghdad," I say.

"What if something happened to you? Your mother would kill me. *My* mother would kill me."

I look out the lobby window. Derek has his arm around Summer's shoulders.

"It's bad enough you blew off your friends and fellow techies . . . ," Reach says.

He points outside. The whole crew is watching us.

"But you also lied to my face about that actor."

"I didn't lie."

He looks at the cup of gelato melting in my hands.

"You said you'd drop it, and you didn't. That's called lying," he says.

I look out the window again. Summer and Derek are gone along with the actors.

Reach sighs.

"I'm sorry to tell you this, but girls like that don't fall for guys like us," Reach says. "At best we're the funny friend. They cry and put their heads on our shoulders when they're having problems. The next day our shirt smells like shampoo, and we think we got some."

"You're wrong," I say.

But I can't be sure. What if Reach is right?

"I'm trying to protect you," Reach says.

"Who asked you to protect me?"

"If it weren't for me, you'd still be up on that ladder."

"That's not true," I say.

"Who got you into tech in the first place?" Reach says. "Who was there for you when your dad—"

He stops himself.

The lobby is empty now. A man with white hair sweeps in the corner of the room.

"It's not even the stupid actor. It's the principle of the thing," Reach says. "We used to be inseparable. We hung out after school every day. We played PlayStation."

"That wasn't so long ago," I say.

"Dude, that was PS2! That's, like, ancient history. I got an iPad. You haven't even seen it."

"Come on. We're not ten years old anymore."

"Since you left, I have to hang out with Half Crack."

"He's cool."

"He sucks! The guy can't even buy pants that fit. How am I going to trust him with state secrets?"

Reach points outside the window. Half Crack is picking his nose.

"It's impossible to get you to do anything," he says. "It's been impossible for a long time, but I keep trying. I know you lost your father, but I lost my best friend."

Anger flares inside me.

"Don't talk about my father," I say. "He has nothing to do with it."

"He has everything to do with it. I spent a year trying to get you down from the ceiling, and then this idiot actor comes along, and five seconds later you're eating gelato. You don't even like gelato!"

"I like it," I say.

"You told me you hated it!" Reach says.

"I never tried it before."

The white-haired man sweeps his way across the room, coming closer to us.

"What do you want me to do?" I say.

"Nothing," Reach says. "I'm finished with you. You want to throw in with the actors? You think they'll accept you? Good luck."

"Wait a second—" I say.

"You lied and you turned your back on me. Now I'm returning the favor."

Reach goes outside, slamming the door behind him.

He says something to the techies, waving one long arm in the air in front of him. The techies look at me, then back at him. Back and forth like they're watching a tennis match.

Reach stops talking.

Half Crack gives me a last look, then turns his back.

Then Benno.

I try to meet Grace's eye, but she won't look at me either. She turns her back like everyone else.

One by one they all turn their backs. A silent protest through glass.

They stay like that for what seems like forever. Then Reach gives the signal, and they walk away.

I wait for Reach to turn back around and motion for me to follow like he always does. But that doesn't happen. Not this time.

The old man in the lobby sweeps his way over to me.

"The show's over," he says. "It's time to go home."

HELENA, ADIEU.

I walk into the theater the next day hoping things blew over during the night. I want Reach to run over when he sees me and say, "I'm sorry, Z. Let's let bygones be bygones." Then he'll give me one of his bony hugs and the techies will stream out onto the stage and all will be forgotten.

If I had stopped to think about it, I'd know it was a ridiculous idea, but it's like my brain refuses to believe what happened at the movie theater. Suspension of disbelief.

I'm barely through the door when Half Crack brushes past me like I don't exist. He doesn't say a word, not even a hello grunt like techies do sometimes when they're busy.

He's the first, but not the last.

Nobody will talk to me. I get dirty looks and cold shoulders. Nothing else. I step into the Cave, and my eye drifts over to the Techie Wall of Fame.

Something's wrong.

There's a blank square next to Reach where my face used to be. I look around the floor just in case my photo fell down. Sometimes tape gets old and yellow and loses its adhesive quality.

But it's not on the floor. It's gone. They've taken it down.

That's when I know it's for real.

I've been exiled.

As I'm walking back to the stage, I notice the emergency door is propped open with cables snaking outside. I peek my head out, and I find Benno and Half Crack hunched over the power box with tools scattered around them.

"What are you doing? You're going to get yourselves killed," I say.

Half Crack reaches into the box.

It's not just any box. It's where the power supply comes into the school building from the electric company.

"We're not supposed to talk to you," Benno says.

"You're not talking to me. You're just answering a question," I say.

"Derek wants us to wire extra dimmers into the cam locks," Half Crack says.

Benno nudges him. "Shut up, dude."

They're talking about tapping into the main power flowing into the building. I know there's a way to do it safely, but I've never done it. None of us has.

"That doesn't make sense," I say.

"The boss wants more light. A fog machine, too," Half Crack says. "And what the boss wants . . ."

He bends over, staring into the power box. Half Crack bending over is not a pretty sight on the best of days, but watching him bend over while messing with three-phase power with enough juice to fry him is particularly frightening.

"When you say *boss*, who are you talking about?" I say.

"Derek is taking charge of the show," Half Crack says.

"He can't do that."

"Who's going to stop him?" Benno says. "Apple's not around. We took a vote on the way home from the movies last night."

I run into the theater.

Derek is pacing back and forth onstage, Ignacio following close behind taking notes on a clipboard.

It's true. Derek made his move.

It's like *Throne of Blood*.

I look for Reach, but he's not around.

"I want us in places in twenty minutes," Derek says to Ignacio.

"Twenty minutes, please!" Ignacio shouts to the theater, relaying the order.

Derek heads towards the stairs on the side of the stage. As he walks past, he pauses.

"How are you today, Z?" he says. It seems like he's in a great mood.

He leans towards me, his mouth right up to my ear.

"I told you I was going to direct," he whispers. "It just happened sooner than I imagined."

He gives my shoulder a little pat, then hops off the stage and takes the director's seat at the tech table.

"Can I talk to you for a minute?" Summer says.

I turn around to find her standing there. She's in costume, her skin pale and beautiful.

"You're the only one who *will* talk to me," I say.

"Privately," Summer says.

Her face is serious. She leads me out to the hall, through the theater department, and into the music area. She doesn't stop until we're safely inside a practice room with the door closed. I feel this burst of excitement, like we're going to rewind and continue the kiss moment from last night, only this time we won't get interrupted.

"I hope I didn't get you in too much trouble last night," she says.

"The techies are blackballing me."

"The actors aren't thrilled with me either."

"I was hoping they'd adopt us as the new 'it' couple," I say.

Summer doesn't laugh.

A viola begins playing in the next room. High-pitched scales.

"That was a joke," I say.

"The thing about the actors—I need them to like me. Especially now."

"They do like you," I say.

"Maybe they do," she says. "But they don't like you, Ziggy. I'm sorry to be so blunt, but they think you're trying to ruin the show. You caused the blackout and that's why Miranda took a nose dive—"

"That's ridiculous."

"I know it is. But think how it looks. I get the lead because Miranda's injured, and then I'm hanging out with the guy who did it?"

"I didn't do it."

"It doesn't matter if you did it or not. It's all perception."

"Why didn't you say any of this before?"

"I didn't think of it before."

"So where did you get this new perspective?" I say.

"People."

She looks down when she says it, which tells me that it's not people.

It's person.

With accent.

"It doesn't matter where I got it," she says. "What

matters is the show. I need them on my side. We have to pull it together fast. Derek needs us."

I was right. Person.

The viola plays, the scales getting higher and higher with each repetition.

"What I mean is, we can't hang out anymore. Not that we'd have time anyway with the production. Do you understand what I'm trying to say?"

"I understand."

Her shoulders relax.

"I'm so relieved," she says.

"Don't worry about me," I say.

She touches my arm, but it's not the same as last night. Last night felt like a beginning touch. This is an ending touch.

"We can still be friends, right?" she says.

The viola stops.

Friends.

Reach was right. I was kidding myself thinking Summer and I might be together. She never cared about me. She was scared about the show, and she needed help. A shoulder to lean on.

A friend.

Just like Reach said. That's all I was to her.

A funny, zitty friend.

I stare at Summer's neck. It looks like there's a red

spot there, probably a zit or a makeup rash, but maybe something else. Maybe a mark.

Maybe Derek's mark.

"You look upset," she says.

"I'm not upset."

I'm staring at her neck. I can't help myself.

"Yes, you are. I see it on your face," she says.

"Stop looking at my face," I say. "I'm not like you, Summer. I don't want people looking at me, applauding for me, whatever. I don't even want them to see me. I like to be away from everyone."

"Okay," she says. "Don't get angry."

"I want to be away from you, too," I say.

The viola starts up again in the next room, a mournful screech that pierces through the wall.

"I have to go," I say, and I run out of the room.

LOVERS AND MADMEN HAVE SUCH SEETHING BRAINS.

When I get to the catwalk, I pop the boomerang and pull my gels out of the spotlight. I check the light plot for Derek's original color choices, the simple ones, the ones I hate. I search the gel sheets until I find them. I take the box cutter from my belt and flick it open.

Now is the time to concentrate. That's the techie first commandment. When you're on a ladder, when a saw is in operation, when you're dealing with electricity, when a blade comes out—Rule One is, everything else goes away and you focus only on the task at hand.

I look at the blade in my fist. I try to follow the rule, focusing on only the knife and the job I'm about to do. I want to feel the healthy fear that makes your senses sharp and keeps you out of trouble.

I try, but I can't feel anything.

I cut the gel, watching the blade slice through the red

poly. I slide the circle of color into the frame and lock it in place with a brad.

"May I have your attention, ladies and gentlemen," Derek says from the tech table below. "I'd like to run Summer's scenes from the top."

I slam the breach closed and jam my finger.

I expect to yelp in pain and jump back, but I don't.

Instead I think about last night. I imagine Summer getting into Derek's beamer, their long ride back to New Jersey. The things they talked about. The things they did.

I grab the gel and throw it to the catwalk. I scrunch up the gel sheet, ruining it forever. Ten dollars down the drain. Maybe fifteen. Derek's donation, his father's money, crushed in my hand.

I grab my phone and call Josh. My finger does it automatically.

"Hey, what's up?" The familiar message starts. I let the message roll through its stupid joke, and then I start to talk.

"Josh, it's Adam." I sniffle, junk filling my nose.

Don't cry, I tell myself. *Josh hates it when you cry.*

"Sorry to call again," I say into the phone, "but I really, really need to talk to you." I suck air too hard, covering the phone with my hand so Josh won't hear it.

"I have to talk to you about what's going on here. I'm

confused, Josh. So if you could call me back, I would appreciate it. Okay?"

I hear myself begging, and it makes me sick inside.

I hang up. I look down at the catwalk. The box cutter is there by my feet.

I wonder what it would feel like to cut myself with it. Not stab myself, just cut along my arm. Would it be crisp like cutting into an apple? Smooth like cutting gel? Or would it be something else, something soft and strange like I've never felt before?

I want to cut myself.

But I don't do it.

I want to hurt someone.

But I don't.

I want to cry.

I don't cry. I never cry.

"Summer darling, are you ready?" Derek asks in the house below.

I close the knife, slip it back into its holster.

I take my place behind the spot.

I flip on the power, feel the machine hum to life in my hands.

Summer steps onstage.

"*O, I am out of breath in this fond chase!*" she says, panting and beautiful, as if she's been running through the woods forever, chasing after love.

IN CHOICE HE IS SO OFT BEGUILED.

First we run Summer's scenes to give her extra practice, and then we take a break and set up to run the entire play from beginning to end. It's the Final Dress—full props, lights, costumes. In a perfect world, the show would be amazing at this point, 90 percent there with the last 10 percent set to appear on opening night.

Bad news.

We're not at 90 percent. Not by a long shot.

Good news.

We're better.

There's a lot more energy. Summer is more comfortable onstage, and she knows her lines. You can feel the actors pulling for her, banding together to try and make it work.

The trip to the city changed something.

Nobody falls, no one quits. There are no blackouts,

freak-outs, or anything else dramatic. The only drama is Shakespeare. Just like it's supposed to be.

I work the spot like a pro. Warnings come over the headset, and I get ready. My cue is called, and I execute. I set for the next one and wait.

I stay focused.

I keep the light on the actors.

That's my job, right?

To put light on people and make them look good. Just like Reach said.

The rehearsal ends, and Derek steps forward.

"I told you last night that a day could sink or save a realm . . . ," he says.

The actors are quiet, waiting.

"I believe this realm has been saved."

Relief floods the room.

The actors applaud each other, and then they applaud Derek. He applauds them back.

It's so perfect, it's sickening.

After things settle down, Derek starts to give notes like a director does.

I see what's happening. He's taking credit for the improvement, and all because of a stupid field trip.

I stop listening.

Later Derek calls the techies into the Cave for their own notes session, but I skip it.

I stay up on the catwalk.

I turn off the spot, leave the fan running through its cool-down cycle. I stow the tools, make sure the instruments are ready for the show tomorrow. I run my final checklist, and then I sit down.

The techie meeting breaks up, and they drift off.

The fan blows.

Nobody talks to me.

A few minutes later, Ignacio comes out, pulling the ghost light downstage center.

"Oh, I didn't see you there," he says.

At first I think he's talking to me, but then Mr. Apple says, "I heard there was a rehearsal."

Ignacio stares at the floor.

"Um . . . yeah," he says.

"How did it go?" Mr. Apple says.

"You know . . ."

"I don't know. Tell me," Mr. Apple says.

"It was a lot better," Ignacio says like he's expecting to get his head bitten off.

"Excellent," Mr. Apple says. "You can head out. And Ignacio—you didn't see me here."

"Yes, sir."

Ignacio shuffles offstage.

Mr. Apple sits in the special place where he watches the show during performances, two seats that have been removed from the very back corner of the audience and replaced with a small bench.

He sighs. "My, my, my," he says.

He stares at the empty stage like he sees something there. He even laughs to himself a few times. I'm afraid the actors were right. He had a nervous breakdown, and now he's pacing and talking to himself like a heavyset Hamlet.

After a while he says: "Are you up there, Mr. Ziegler?"

"I'm up here," I say. "How did you know?"

"You're always up there."

"Not always. But often," I say.

Mr. Apple chuckles.

"You're probably wondering if I'm going crazy," he says.

"The thought crossed my mind."

"You know that expression—he saw his life flash before his eyes?"

"Yes."

"I'm watching my career flash before my eyes."

"I'm sorry."

"Don't be. It's a short flash."

Mr. Apple takes Carol Channing from his lap and puts her on the ground so she can walk around.

"The associate principal is out for blood. He's been trying to get rid of me for years, and now he's got evidence aplenty. I may have lost both my teaching and directing careers. When God cleans house, he doesn't fool around."

"What will you do?"

Mr. Apple shrugs.

"Maybe I'll become a techie," he says with a laugh.

"I'll show you the ropes," I say.

"You're a good lad," he says. "I wish I could join you up there, but I haven't been on a catwalk in more than a decade."

I try to imagine Mr. Apple climbing a ladder, but I can't. It would defy the laws of physics.

"It's not easy being big," Mr. Apple says. "Sylvester wants me to get lap-band, but I've got an unnatural fondness for my stomach. Why would I give a portion of it to science?"

He waves his hand in the air like he's blowing away smoke.

"Maybe I just love food too much. I love a lot of things too much," he says.

"But not the theater," I say.

"The theater most of all."

"You said you hated it."

"Hate, love. You're too young to know how closely related they are."

"I know a lot more than you think," I say to Mr. Apple.

"Fair enough," Mr. Apple says. "Do you know I've spent my entire life in the theater? It started when I was ten years old. I did a play in camp, a musical called *Pippin*. Seldom performed now, but quite famous in its day. It was my first production, and it was extraordinary. Not the show itself. That was decent, nothing more. But the theater. Being onstage. That was extraordinary. I was ten years old, but I knew right away. Theater was the greatest drug in the world."

I think about how it feels to see my light onstage. The instruments I've chosen and the angles where I've set them up. Then the actors and costumes are added, and it becomes a dance of light, movement, and color.

Mr. Apple is right. It's the best feeling in the world.

"I started theater two years ago," I say. "Reach got me into it."

"You love being a techie."

"I used to. It's a little rough right now. Actually, it's very rough."

Mr. Apple sighs.

"It's sad when you fall out of love," he says.

"I'm not sure what happened," I say.

"In *or* out. They both twist you into a pretzel."

I shift on the catwalk, lying on my belly so I can look at Mr. Apple through the grating.

"It sounds like rehearsal went well tonight," Mr. Apple says.

"It went better, but not well."

"Shakespeare has survived for nearly four hundred years. This production is unlikely to destroy him."

Mr. Apple puts his hands on his thighs and pushes himself to standing.

"You can't quit, Mr. Apple. What if something happens? Derek won't know what to do."

"The show will go on."

"You can't quit!" I say.

I jump to my feet. I run across the catwalk to the ladder.

"Be careful," Mr. Apple shouts.

"Please, Mr. Apple. We need you."

I start down, climbing fast, afraid Mr. Apple will leave before I make it to the bottom.

"Lad. Lad."

I stumble on the last rung and catch myself. I make it to the theater floor and run over to Mr. Apple.

"You can't go!" I say.

He looks at me, surprised.

"What's all this about?"

"I care about people, and it doesn't matter. They break up with me or we have a fight or something bad happens to them."

"I don't understand," Mr. Apple says.

I try to stop myself, but the words keep coming.

"Everyone leaves, Mr. Apple. You can't leave, too."

"I'm sorry, lad. I've already left. I just came to say good-bye."

I bite down on my lip.

"I think you have a lot going on right now," Mr. Apple says.

He uses that quiet voice that people use when they're worried about you. Or they think you're going crazy.

"Do you have someone you can talk to?" he says.

I think about Josh. Reach. Mom.

There's no one really. Nobody who understands.

"Yes," I say to Mr. Apple.

"Good," Mr. Apple says. "Then I must bid you *adieu*."

He looks around the theater, tips an invisible hat to the air, and says:

"And *adieu* to you, dear lady."

He bows deeply and stays there for a long time, his head down, his arm tucked in at his waist.

I want to look away, but I can't.

He slowly comes back to standing. He gestures to the theater walls.

"I gave her all I had," he says. "And it wasn't enough."

He whistles for Carol Channing. She runs up to him but refuses to jump into his arms. She circles him twice then heads for the door on her own, prancing on tiny paws.

"Women," he says with a sigh.

"No kidding," I say.

He tips the invisible hat to me and goes out.

The theater doors click shut behind him.

The ghost light flickers.

I imagine the bulb burning, leaving me alone here in a dark theater.

I start to feel afraid.

I should go home now. I should call someone, like Mr. Apple said.

But I don't.

I climb.

I DO HEAR THE MORNING LARK.

I wake to a ringing sound.

It's not my alarm. It's the morning school bell.

I'm on the catwalk in the dark theater.

I check my phone, see the texts between me and Mom. Then I remember. I fell asleep in the theater and woke up after an hour. I sent Mom a text saying I was staying at Reach's house and went back to sleep.

I hear students moving through the school, laughing and messing around in the hall. It's like a party through a wall, far away and muted.

I look at the date. May 20. Opening night.

I should go to my first class, but I don't move.

It's daytime, but no real light makes it into the theater. There is only the ghost light standing guard against the gloom.

I look down at the stage.

A light goes on in my head. Not one of Derek's lights.

A different light.

I imagine it glowing in a corner, a pale amber that streams across the back of the stage, spreading up the wide arc of the cyclorama.

It is a beginning.

In my head I paint the stage with other lights, dabbing in orange muted with brown.

I pick a focal point and lay in a soft golden light with a hot center, diffuse around the edges. I let red seep in from the top.

I look at the palette I've created in my head.

Sunrise.

I recognize the colors and the way they're mixed.

My father's style, mixed in light rather than paint.

I lay back on the catwalk and let the light wash over me. I cover myself with a jacket, and I close my eyes. I know it's dark, but the light in my imagination is warm and familiar.

I spend the entire day up on the catwalk. I don't eat or drink anything so I don't have to go to the bathroom. I just lie on the catwalk all day thinking about my life. I think about Dad, how everything would be okay if he were still here. I know it's a lie. Everything wasn't perfect when Dad was alive. But it's hard to believe they wouldn't be perfect now if he were here.

My phone buzzes every hour or so. I glance at it time

and again, hoping it might be Summer calling, or Reach, or even Josh calling me back. But it never is.

It's Mom. Nervous texting. Her specialty.

I respond to her: *sho-day. bzy. c u 2nite.*

Okay, sweetie pie. I will see you at the show, she texts.

The messages stop.

And I start thinking again.

For the next couple hours, people wander in and out of the theater. There are final set and light checks. Props and wardrobe people come and go.

Bells chime at the end of each period, but I don't pay attention. I'm waiting for the day to end, even though I have no idea what I'll do then.

"Knock, knock," Grace says.

I turn to find Grace's head peeking over the edge of the catwalk. "I didn't hear you climbing."

"I'm sneaky like that," she says. "Can I come up?"

"I guess."

She climbs onto the catwalk. She's a natural in the air, not like Reach, who hates it up here.

"I couldn't sleep last night," she says. "I kept thinking about what happened, and then I got cramps and had to use the toilet, like, fourteen times."

"Spare me the details."

"I'm just saying I was upset. I hate that I turned my back on you."

"Reach can be very persuasive."

"It's got nothing to do with Reach. It's about you. I was angry at you."

"Because I blew everyone off?"

"Because you blew me off."

I look at her, confused.

"What am I missing?" I say.

"You blew me off for that stupid actress."

"What does that have to do with us?"

"You're crazy about her!" Grace says, and she grunts and buries her face in her hands.

"Grace?"

"I'm so stupid," she says.

"You're in love with Derek, aren't you?" I say.

"I thought I was. But I started having different thoughts."

"What kinds of thoughts?"

"Like maybe Derek is an old story."

"What's the new story?"

"You and me," she says.

"I don't believe it."

"It's just that you were so nice to me, and then we were in the beamer, and we had so much fun—"

"It was fun for me, too," I say.

"And I thought, if it was fun once, maybe it would be fun again. Or fun for a long time."

I think about Grace grinding through the gears in the beamer. The super serious look on her face. It makes me smile to think of it.

Grace says, "It's not like I'm in love with you or anything. I just thought maybe . . . maybe we had a chance of becoming something."

"You were so preoccupied with Derek. I never thought about us that way."

"I was preoccupied," she says. "But things change. You have to move on."

"I know," I say. But how do you do that?

Grace sits cross-legged on the catwalk across from me.

"What about you and me?" she says.

"Bad timing," I say.

"Bummer," she says.

We watch the people come and go down below us.

"You know that actress—she gave me the *just friends* speech."

"I hate that speech," Grace says.

"No kidding."

"How do you feel?"

"How did it feel with Derek?"

"Like liquid hell."

"It's like that. Only the liquid is boiling."

"I'm sorry," Grace says.

"How long does it last?"

"No way to know. You just have to ride it out. Try not to go crazy."

"I already went crazy."

"How crazy?"

"I almost cried in front of Mr. Apple."

"That's not so crazy."

"I slept in the theater last night."

"Did you wear a mask and play the organ?"

"Not yet."

"Resist the impulse. That would be crazy."

The school bell rings, and the hall fills with voices.

"Why are you here in the middle of the day?" I say.

"They let us out of class a little early so we could get ready for the show."

A bunch of cast members gather in the front of the theater.

"I should get my act together," Grace says.

"I'm going to stay up here."

"If you need anything—" I hold up my phone. "I'm adding you to my favorites list," I say.

"You're already on mine," she says.

She winks and heads down the ladder, joining the cast and crew assembling onstage.

The theater doors burst open. Derek enters with a flourish.

"Ladies and gentlemen," he says. "It's showtime!"

THAT NIGHT
WE PLAY OUR PLAY.

"Stand by to fade house," Ignacio says on the headset.

"Standing by," Benno says.

"Let me have your attention, everyone. Derek would like to say a few words."

There's a scraping sound as Ignacio turns his headset over to Derek.

"Tech folk, I'd like to thank you in advance for a superb job. It's a great honor to be helming this, my first show."

Helming? He didn't direct this show. He just stepped in at the last rehearsal.

Derek says, "I'd like to dedicate this performance to the memory of Mr. Apple, our beloved mentor."

The sound of mics being clicked on and off. Techie applause.

My stomach churns. Mr. Apple isn't dead. Derek is creating this story to make himself look like a hero.

"Break a leg," Derek says.

More mics clicking.

Ignacio comes back on the line. "Let's do it. House to zero."

"House to zero," Benno repeats.

The lights fade to black, and I flip on a penlight and close my fist around it. I hold my glowing hand up to my face.

The buzz in the audience dies down. Nine hundred people sit in silence, waiting for the show to begin. Then the stage lights come up, the instruments creaking around me as the metal comes to temperature.

Tom, the super tall actor playing Theseus, steps out.

TOM

Now, fair Hippolyta, our nuptial hour

Draws on apace; four happy days bring in

Another moon . . .

Four days.

It was only four days ago that I saw Summer for the first time dancing in the hallway.

My whole life changed. Then it fell apart. And it only took four days.

I want to quit the show. Right now in the middle of everything. Climb down the ladder and walk out the door. Leave the theater forever like Mr. Apple.

The techies hate me. The actors hate me. My best friend won't talk to me.

Summer is gone forever.

And once again, Derek is a star.

Why stay on crew? There's nothing left for me here.

Summer steps out onstage. She's in full costume and makeup, her face shining and beautiful.

"Stand by for spot," Ignacio says over my headset.

The spot.

I still have my light.

The thought alone gives me hope.

"Stand by for fog," Ignacio says.

Fog?

We didn't do fog at dress rehearsal.

I think about Benno and Half Crack messing with the cam locks behind the theater. Did they install the extra dimmers?

SUMMER

How happy some o'er other some can be!

"Spot, *go*," Ignacio says. "Fog, *go*."

There's a hissing sound as fog is released onto the stage.

I pre-focus the spot, aim towards Summer, and flip on the fan.

I push the button to spark the light.

There's a buzzing sound, followed by a loud *pop*—

At first I think it's my lamp that's blown, but then I see that the stage lights are out, too.

The entire theater is black.

"What the hell is going on?" I hear Reach say in my headset.

"Benno, did you hit the blackout switch?" I say.

"I don't know what happened," Benno says.

I imagine him panicking in the booth. I count the five long seconds it will take for him to figure out what happened, reset the cue, and get the lights up.

My count hits five, and nothing changes.

By seven, I know we're in trouble.

At ten, I hear Ignacio's voice, frazzled and desperate, over the headset.

"Bring the lights back up," he says.

"The computer isn't responding," Benno says.

Reach cuts in: "Try shutting down the power. That will reset the system."

"Everything's dead," Benno says. He's so upset he's slurring his words.

I scan the theater, checking for the familiar red glow of the backstage work lights. Those are the tiny lamps that provide just enough light for the actors to find their way offstage.

There's no red glow; that means the power is blown for the entire theater.

It's been fifteen seconds, and the audience is shifting in their seats. People are whispering.

"Reach, flip the breakers," I say.

"On it," he says. There's no argument from him now, no personal issues. The techies are in emergency mode. That's what it means to be a pro. You put your crap aside.

"Everybody keep it together!" Ignacio says.

That's when the bad feeling starts in my chest.

I think of the theater filled to capacity, nine hundred people in the pitch-black, with me alone above them.

But I am not alone. My father is next to me.

He doesn't speak, doesn't reach for me. But I can sense him there, next to me on the catwalk.

The audience murmurs below. Voices whispering in the dark.

It's early morning, and I'm awakened by strange voices murmuring in the other room.

I'm in New Hampshire, the cottage where we spent our summers.

I'm annoyed because they woke me up. Even more annoyed because I can't get back to sleep. I open the door and walk into the living room, ready to yell at my parents for talking loudly so early in the morning.

I see the uniforms first.

My mother sits alone on the couch. Two police officers stand in front of her.

My father is not there.

Back in the theater, my breath quickens, my heart beating rapidly in my chest.

"There's no power coming into the theater," Reach says in the headset.

I reach for my father next to me on the catwalk, but he stands a few steps away, just out of arms reach.

"Dad," I say.

He doesn't respond. He stands there, an outline barely visible in the darkness.

The dark.

My father loved light. He loved talking about it, thinking about it, painting it. He loved looking at light.

And he died in the dark.

I remember now. This thing that haunts me in my dreams then disappears when I'm awake.

The reason the police were in the house talking to Mom. I remember now.

"Your dad's car was found in the woods outside of Concord," they said. "Single car accident. He drove off the road on the way home."

It's not like I ever forget it.

I just don't want to think about it. So I put it out of my mind.

"His car was spotted from the road by a passing cruiser. He went down a gulley then traveled several feet into the woods before hitting a tree," one officer said.

"You could barely see it from the road," the other one said.

"It's easy to do on that stretch. No guardrails. A narrow road with gravel on either side."

"That's why we couldn't find him until morning."

The crash was bad, but he did not die instantly. They didn't tell Mom that. I read it later in the coroner's report. Time of death estimated between four and seven a.m. Which means Dad spent the night stuck in the car, trapped and bleeding.

I think about him alone in the middle of the night, in pain, waiting for dawn to come. I wonder if he saw the sunrise.

I'll never know.

I only know that since that morning two years ago, I hate the dark.

"I think we blew the transformer," Ignacio says. "There's no power in the building."

I look behind me at the front doors of the theater. I should be able to see a faint glow along the crack beneath the door. There's nothing. The hall lights are out, too.

"We have to evacuate the theater," Ignacio says.

"No!" Derek says. "My father is out there!"

The audience is talking now, some of them getting up

to find their way out of the theater by the light of their cell phones. They make it halfway up the aisle and get stuck. A couple of kids are crying. An audience member shouts at the stage: "What's going on!"

Chaos is about to erupt. It could be bad, even dangerous.

"You're a techie. Do something!" I hear Derek say on the headphones, followed by the chatter of techie voices backstage.

It's a disaster.

There's no light, and now there's no show.

I look for Dad's image in the darkness, but he's gone.

QUICK BRIGHT THINGS.

I pull a glow stick from my pocket, bend it until it cracks, and shake it hard.

I remember one time Dad and I went out into the woods at night, and he cut open a glow stick and shook it onto a tree. Dad wanted me to see how the chemicals still glowed outside the tube. He used them like paint, transforming the dark woods into a green speckled abstract.

The woods.

Most of *Midsummer* takes place in the woods.

I have an idea. I could cut open glow sticks and sprinkle them on the fairies. I imagine them moving across the stage like they're walking through the woods at night, seen and not seen.

That image is followed by another: flashlight beams crossing the woods at night. You turn the beam on someone's face, and you're expecting it to be one person, but it's someone else. Maybe the person was your friend, but now they're your enemy. Or the person you thought loved you is gone forever, replaced by a stranger.

Something clicks for me, something essential about the meaning of the play.

It's so confusing in the woods at night, you can't be sure if you're awake or dreaming.

That idea triggers a rush of images, ways I can light the show. All of them use stuff we have backstage. None of it has to be plugged in.

The audience is calling out now, shouting at the stage, demanding to know what's going on. Most people have turned on their phones. I see faces glowing blue in the darkness.

"Ladies and gentlemen, please stay calm," Ignacio says. He stumbles onstage with an electric lantern, waving his hand to help disperse the fog.

A lantern. I could use a lantern, too.

"Can I have your attention, please," Ignacio says. "We've had a power outage. I'm sorry but we have to cancel the show—"

I need to do something. I can't let it end like this.

I tuck the glow stick in the collar of my shirt and navigate to the ladder at the edge of the catwalk. I look into the darkness below.

I take a deep breath, and I climb.

Ignacio says, "For your own safety, we ask you to remain in your seats until we can get some lights up. Then we'll lead you out of the theater."

The audience groans.

"Hail, Mortals!" I shout from the middle of the ladder.

The audience turns in their seats to see who's talking.

I flip on the flashlight beam.

"What are you doing, Z?" Ignacio calls to me from the stage.

The audience chuckles uncomfortably, not understanding what's going on.

I use the big Mag like a spotlight, swinging it from one face to another until I have the audience's attention. The light hits my mom, her mouth frozen in amazement.

I navigate down the center aisle and hop onstage, walking past Ignacio.

I mash a couple of Shakespeare's lines together: *"And now from depths of darkest night / Through the house give gathering light!"*

And I hand the Maglite to Summer.

"You look like you could use a light," I say.

"Thank you," Summer says.

The audience laughs.

"What do I do with this?" she whispers.

"Use it as part of the scene."

"You want me to improvise Shakespeare?"

"You texted me Shakespeare."

"That was different."

"You can do it," I say.

"How do you know?"

She bites at her lip with her front tooth, just like she did that night at my house. She thinks hard for a second, and then her face relaxes.

"I'll try it," she says. She points the light at different places around the stage.

"'Tis dark in the forest," she says. "Methinks a girl could get lost out here."

"Hey, what about a light for me?" Wesley says.

"Ah yes, m'lord," I say.

I take out a penlight and hand it to him.

He looks down at the tiny light, and the audience howls with laughter.

"*Crewus technicalis!* We need more light!" I shout, and I wave my glow stick towards the wings, signaling Reach.

I take the lantern away from Ignacio and place it on the front lip of the stage so the actors know where the edge is.

"You can't do this," Ignacio says.

"Do you have a better idea?" I say.

He glances at the audience, embarrassed.

"You have to talk to Derek," he whispers. "Chain of command."

He stamps his way offstage, tripping on a ramp and nearly going down.

I hear a noise from offstage. Reach rushes out from the wings with an armful of flashlights.

"*Crewus technicalis* at your service," he says with a bow.

The audience laughs again.

"Thank God," I whisper.

"I'm doing it for the show," he says. "Not for you."

"For the show," I say. "That's reason enough."

We pass the flashlights out to the actors.

"What are we supposed to do with these?" Johanna whispers.

"Start the lines," I say. "Don't move around a lot. Stay together and use the flashlights to help you."

"This is crazy," Wesley says.

"Let's try it," Summer says. "It's like an improv exercise."

She steps forward, turns the light up towards her face, and says:

SUMMER

```
Love looks not with the eyes, but with the mind;
   And therefore is wing'd Cupid painted blind.
```

And the play begins again.

BEHIND UNSEEN.

I walk backstage into chaos. Derek is yelling at the techies, the actors clumped around him. He whirls around when he sees me.

"What do you think you're doing?" Derek says.

"I'm trying to save the show."

"It's not your show to save."

"I have an idea," I say.

"Can you get the lights back on?" he says.

"I don't think so, but I can—"

"I don't want to hear it," Derek says.

"I want to hear it," Mr. Apple says.

Everyone turns.

Mr. Apple is standing in the door of the cave with colored glow bracelets strung around his neck and arms. He looks like a Mardi Gras float.

"Mr. Apple. Have you been here all along?" Derek says.

Mr. Apple shrugs.

"I wanted to see the show," he says. "I couldn't stay away."

"We had some kind of technical glitch," Derek says. "I don't know what happened, but I believe the techies are responsible."

"Now is not the time for blame," Mr. Apple says. "Now is the time for inspiration."

Mr. Apple looks from Derek back to me.

"What do you think, Mr. Ziegler?"

Derek sneers at me.

"I don't know," I say.

"You knew enough to come down that ladder and get the show started again," Mr. Apple says. "What happens next?"

"Nothing happens next," Derek says. "We call the fire department to evacuate, and we reschedule the opening until everything is fixed and we can do the play the way it's supposed to be done. Fully designed."

"Mr. Ziegler?" Mr. Apple says.

Everyone is watching me. The techies and actors, Derek and Ignacio.

I should keep quiet, let Derek do whatever he wants.

But that's how I always do it.

I look towards Reach, and he gives me the tiniest nod. It's dark, so I can't be sure it happened. Then he does it again. Really subtle, so nobody but me can see.

Go for it.

And I do. I lean in towards Mr. Apple and I try to describe the play I have in my head.

"I think we should sprinkle glow sticks on the fairies," I say. "And Puck should have a miner's helmet. And we can use flashlights in the forest scenes. And we can give the actors glow bracelets like you're wearing, Mr. Apple."

I'm waiting for Apple to shoot me down, but he doesn't. He lets me get it all out.

I finish and there's silence. People are looking at me, but I can't tell what they're thinking, whether I've made an idiot out of myself or not.

"See what I mean?" Derek says. "Ridiculous ideas."

"Do it," Mr. Apple says to me.

"What do you mean, do it? What about the fire code?" Derek says.

"Mr. Dunkirk, I'd like to speak to you alone please."

Mr. Apple puts a hand on Derek's shoulder and leads him away.

I turn to the techies.

"Grace, get all the actors into the Cave. That will be our base of operations. Benno, collect the emergency flashlights from the classrooms. Half Crack, get the carton of glow sticks from the back shelf in wardrobe. What else do we have that makes light?"

"I've got lanterns in the props room," Reach says.

I snap a glow stick and hand it to him.

"Grab whatever you can," I say. "Lay a path from backstage onto the stage so the actors can find their way. Meet back in five minutes."

"I'm proud of you," he says.

"This could be a disaster," I say.

"Whatever happens," he says, "you stood up."

And he rushes into the darkness.

THE STORY SHALL BE CHANGED.

It's too dangerous for the actors to go onto the set pieces, so scene after scene plays out on the few feet of stage floor in front of the set. Every design element that Derek built—all the ladders, pulleys, ramps, and staircases—has to be abandoned. The production is stripped down to nothing but actors and light.

The techies work together backstage keeping the pathways clear, leading actors in and out of the Cave, then walking them onstage so nobody gets hurt.

Mr. Apple and I stand together in the wings making decisions about everything. We decide the fairies should have glow sticks, the humans flashlights, and the actors—Shakespeare calls them mechanicals—glow bracelets and a bunch of lanterns. We give one of the actors a big emergency light, and he uses it like a spotlight on the mechanicals during their rehearsal scenes.

The audience barely stirs during most of the show. They laugh from time to time, which is a good sign, but I can't tell if they're laughing at us or with us. And most of the time it's so quiet I don't know if they're awake or asleep.

The night goes by in a blur, bodies moving in the darkness, actors' faces seen in the beams of the techies' flashlights.

Summer passes me a dozen or more times during the night, but we don't speak again.

I keep hoping she might say something to break the ice, but she never does.

At one point near the end of the show, Johanna finds me backstage.

"Adam, what do you think if Wesley and Peter steal my flashlight in this scene? They're not in love with me anymore, so maybe they just grab it and give it to Summer."

I'm so startled she's talking to me, I don't answer.

"Is it a terrible idea?" she says.

"No, it's a great idea. It's funny," I say.

"Do you think so?"

"Sure. And at the end of the play when things are back to normal, they can return it to you."

"That's great!" she says, and gives me a big smile.

"You're so nice. Why didn't I know this?"

"Because you're always with Reach when you see me. And I'm a bitch when I'm around him."

"But why?"

"You don't know?" she says. "You two are such good friends, I just assumed—"

I shrug.

"Okay, here's the thing," she says. "He asked me out."

"He did not," I say.

"Like a hundred times. I told him I wasn't interested, but he kept sending me cards, notes, even a Vermont Teddy Bear."

"No way," I say.

"The fifteen-inch Chic Shopper Bear. He sewed his name onto its shirt and built a tiny prop Macy's bag because he knows that's my favorite store."

"Holy crap. That does sound like Reach."

"When he wouldn't back off, I had to be mean until he got the message."

Ignacio interrupts us.

"Cue coming up," he whispers.

"So that's the story," she says to me. "Sorry I've been flaming you all year."

"What about the stuff you said a few days ago? Did you really think I sabotaged the show?"

"Honestly? I wasn't sure."

"What do you think now?"

"Now it's obvious," she says.

"We need you onstage," Ignacio says to her.

"What's obvious?" I say.

"You didn't sabotage it. You saved it."

She gives me a quick hug and heads onstage for her scene.

Mr. Apple beckons to me from the Cave.

"I want to give everyone candles for the last scene," he says. "What do you think?"

I imagine the wedding ceremony playing out in candlelight.

"I like it," I say.

"Make it happen," Mr. Apple says.

I grab a bag of tea light candles. Grace, Reach, and I pass out paper plates to put under them so the actors won't burn their hands. Before I know it, we've sent twenty-five actors onstage in a long candlelit procession humming "One Hand, One Heart" from *West Side Story*.

Hubbard, the actor who plays Puck, is last in line. Mr. Apple holds onto her elbow, whispering instructions into her ear. Then he sends her onstage, too.

I turn towards the Cave to make sure we didn't forget anyone, and Derek is there.

"Well played," he says. "This whole evening. Bravo."

"I tried to save the show," I say.

"You did," Derek says. "Tonight you are a hero."

"Thank you," I say.

"But everything we talked about for next year? Forget

it. You'll never get near another light, not as long as I have anything to say about it. And I'm going to have a lot to say, at least according to Mr. Apple. He offered me my own show next year. Can you believe that? Direct and design on the big stage. Recompense for my covering his ass when he freaked out."

"You're going to direct a whole show?" I say.

"A musical," Derek says. "Maybe my production of *Wicked* will finally come to fruition. We shall see."

"Congratulations," I say.

"Thank you so much," he says with a smile. "So enjoy your night, Z. It's a big one for you. Your first lighting design . . . and your last."

Mr. Apple appears with a flashlight in hand.

"Come on, lad," he says to me. "I want you to see this."

He walks me to the wings. I glance back at Derek. I see him grinning at me, his teeth ghostly white in the darkness.

Mr. Apple positions us so we have a view of the stage.

It's beautiful. There are candles everywhere. It doesn't feel like a play at all, more like a celebration at night in someone's backyard.

"Watch this," Mr. Apple says.

The final speech in the play belongs to Puck. Mr. Apple has directed it so the entire cast is onstage, all of them frozen except Puck. Puck comes forward to speak to the audience.

HUBBARD

If we shadows have offended,
Think but this, and all is mended . . .

I never paid attention to the ending much before, but listening to it now makes me angry. It seems like Shakespeare's big apology. He writes a whole play about how you can't trust love, and then at the end he chickens out and ties up the loose ends.

HUBBARD

You have but slumber'd here
While these visions did appear.

I'm not opposed to a happy ending, but how realistic is that? Shakespeare sends Puck out to say, *Sorry if I scared you. Maybe it was all a dream.*

If I believe that, then maybe I believe my life is a dream. I didn't almost get Summer and lose her, Reach isn't mad at me, and Grace's heart isn't broken. Maybe Derek isn't going to destroy me after the show. Maybe I'll get offstage tonight and Dad will be there with Josh and Mom, the three of them laughing and waiting to congratulate me.

My own perfect happy ending.

"Are you watching, lad?" Mr. Apple says.

He puts his hand on my shoulder and squeezes.

I look at the candles spread across the stage, flickering like a field of stars.

I look at Summer, beautiful in candlelight.

It's a perfect moment.

Then Puck walks over to Jazmin—and blows out her candle.

Puck blows out Johanna's. And Wesley's. She continues down the line, blowing out the candles one by one.

This is what Mr. Apple wanted me to see. The fairies are supposed to bless everyone at the end of the play. But Puck is doing the opposite. She's extinguishing each flame.

Mr. Apple has shifted the entire meaning of the play. It's not a story about a world that went wrong for a time then returned to normal. It's more complex than that. Things happen, and who knows why? We have to find a way to deal with it.

I look back at Mr. Apple, and he throws me a wink.

"It's amazing what a little inspiration can do," he says.

"Are you still going to quit?" I say.

"I thought a lot about it," Mr. Apple says. "You know what I realized?"

Puck walks to the front of the stage.

The entire theater is dark now, the audience silent.

There's a single actor. A single candle.

"I'm a theater person," Mr. Apple says. "This is my home."

Puck holds out her candle, scanning the faces of the audience.

HUBBARD

So, good night unto you all . . .

Then something unexpected happens. Candle wax drips on Hubbard's hand, and she shakes it in pain.

Her flame goes out, and the room is cast in total darkness.

I hold my breath.

I wait for the fear to come, but it doesn't.

I look for my father in the dark, but he's not there.

It's just me and Mr. Apple offstage right, standing together.

A cheer rises from the audience. People are applauding wildly, shouting at the stage in excitement.

The rear doors of the theater open, and light floods in from emergency lights the fire department has set up in the hall.

Ignacio motions for the crew to follow him onstage, each one with a flashlight.

I don't join them. I stay backstage and watch.

The audience continues to applaud. First the actors

bow, then the techies, then everyone together.

Some of the techies call my name, just a few at first, then all of them. Soon the actors join in.

"Ad-*am*!" they shout over and over. And a few call out, "Z!"

I listen to the applause, people shouting my name. I look to see if Summer is shouting for me. She's not.

"Are you going out?" Mr. Apple says.

I look over my shoulder. Derek is standing in shadow behind me. I can't see his face, but I can sense him watching me.

"I don't know," I say.

"Enjoy your moment in the spotlight," Mr. Apple says. "You earned it."

He nudges me onto the stage. The techies and actors turn their flashlights on me.

The audience cheers.

I hold my hand up over my face, trying to hide my zits. Then I take it down.

I stand and let everyone see me.

I even take a little bow, and the crowd goes wild.

I think of what Mr. Apple said about the first time he was onstage. I can sort of see why he liked it.

The audience continues to applaud. I take another little bow, and before the applause ends, I walk offstage.

I walk right past the actors and techies, past Derek

and Mr. Apple—straight out the back of the theater. I walk down the hall of the theater department where I first saw Summer. I go out the back door of the school.

The lights of the fire trucks revolve slowly, bouncing red-yellow light across the asphalt.

I walk through the parking lot, and I don't stop until I find Mom's Volvo.

I send her a text, telling her I'm waiting for her at the car.

It's not that I don't like applause. It's kind of nice.

But all those people looking at me—

There's only so much a techie can take.

THEY WILLFULLY THEMSELVES EXILE FROM LIGHT.

"That was amazing," Mom says. "*You* were amazing."

Mom is so excited, she's driving almost thirty miles per hour instead of her usual twenty. We pass Enzo's then turn the corner towards home.

"I didn't do that much. I was backstage most of the time," I say.

"The lights," Mom says. "All those beautiful ideas. You were everywhere up there."

"They were Mr. Apple's ideas, too. We were working together."

"That's the best way. A collaboration."

I look at the headlights on the pavement, the way they reflect off a bank of trees, then disappear into the dark again.

"Do you think about Dad?" I say.

Mom's eyes flit towards me then back to the road.

"What kind of question is that?" she says.

"We never talk about it," I say. "We almost talk about it, but we never do."

Mom stares at the road. I'm waiting for her to ignore my question or change the subject. That's how we usually do it.

"I think of him every day," she says.

"Me, too."

"I know you do."

"I've been afraid to tell you," I say.

"Why afraid?"

"I don't want to make you sad."

"I'm already sad, Adam. We both are. It's a sad thing that happened."

I remember waking up one particular morning after it happened. Not the morning when the police were at the house. And not the morning of the funeral.

Those mornings were terrible, but they were easy in comparison.

This morning was three weeks later.

I slept all night with a flashlight in the crook of my arm. That started right after Dad died, bringing the flashlight to bed with me. I'd been having nightmares for weeks, but this night was different. When I woke up, I felt peaceful for the first time in weeks.

Then I opened my eyes.

It was Monday. The first day of high school. Time for me to start again.

A new school.

A new life.

I opened the blinds in my bedroom, and the morning light burned my eyes.

The universe seemed cruel to me then, the way it can turn out the lights and turn them on again with the flip of a switch. It can turn off the sun. Or a person. Whatever it chooses to do. And you're just supposed to go on as if nothing happened.

I hated everyone that day. Dad for dying. Me for living. And Josh.

"I'm so angry at Josh," I say out loud.

"Why, honey?"

"Dad died and he took off. Now he's having a great life at Cornell."

Mom thinks about that for a second.

"Everyone deals with things in their own way," she says.

"He wasn't even sad. He had a new girlfriend like a week later."

First I lost Dad. Then I lost Josh. That's what it felt like.

Mom bites at her thumbnail.

"I made a lot of mistakes, too," she says.

"No, you didn't."

I think about Mom after it happened. Sleeping until noon, then disappearing into the bathroom for half the day.

"I couldn't handle it," Mom says. "I tried to be there for you, but I drifted into my own world."

"I went backstage," I say.

I started tech in the fall right after Dad died. It seemed like a great thing at the time. New friends, new interests. That's what everyone said I needed to do. That's what Reach said, too, and I didn't disagree.

The theater became my whole life. And then it kind of replaced my life.

Who was I before that?

I try to think back to that time, back when I was thirteen.

What did I like? Who did I want to be?

It seems like it was so long ago.

Then I remember—the cardboard box on the top shelf of my closet. It's been up there for two years, untouched. Forgotten about.

Not completely forgotten.

It's Dad's box, filled with tubes of acrylic paint, palette knives, brushes—

"I wanted to be a painter," I say to Mom.

"That was a long time ago," she says.

"I wanted to be a painter like Dad. After he died, I

couldn't deal with it. I gave up. I got into tech so I wouldn't have to think about it."

"But, honey—you *are* a painter."

"No, I'm not."

"Tonight on that stage. You made a painting with light."

I think about the images from tonight's production. Flashlight beams crisscrossing the woods. Fairies speckled and glowing in the dark. A slow procession of candles.

Mom's right.

My phone vibrates. Right away I think of Josh. What if it's him calling? That would be the perfect ending. He calls to say he's coming home. Tomorrow we'll sit down and talk things out. It's like the scene in the musical where the family hugs at the end, reunited and singing in perfect harmony.

The phone is still vibrating.

I look at the screen.

It's Reach.

I consider not answering, but then I change my mind.

"Are you coming to the cast party?" he says when I answer.

"I wasn't planning on it," I say.

"Well, plan."

I don't say anything.

"Let me rephrase that," Reach says. "It would be cool if you came."

"Why?" I say.

"Giving you the silent treatment sucks," he says.

I hear singing in the background, a cast party in full swing.

"To tell you the truth, I'm kind of lonely without you," Reach says.

That's a good reason. But I don't tell him that.

"Where is it?" I say.

"Derek's House. Upper Mountain Ave."

"Ugh," I say.

I think of Derek holding court in his dad's gigantic house.

"Is he gunning for me?" I say.

"I think he's gunning for other things."

"What kinds of things?"

"Summer," Reach says.

"Okay," I say, and I hang up.

"What was that about?" Mom says.

I look at the road. We're almost home. It would be so easy to let Mom drive me home, go up to my room, lie in bed, and think about the show. I could hear the applause again in my head. I could hug my pillow and dream of lighting Summer.

"Stop," I say to Mom.

"Stop what?"

"Stop the car!"

Mom hits the brake a little too hard.

"I'm not going up to my room," I say.

"I didn't tell you to go to your room."

"I know, I know," I say.

Mom looks confused.

"Can you take me to the cast party?" I say.

IT IS NOT NIGHT WHEN I DO SEE YOUR FACE.

Upper Montclair is a series of expensive homes and more expensive mansions. Mom pulls up in front of one of the mansions. It's not like a castle or anything, but it's huge and every light is on.

"This is a nice place," Mom says.

"Derek's dad is Thomas Dunkirk."

"The architect?"

"That's the one."

The windows are open, and I can hear Peter singing the title song from *Rent* at the top of his lungs. All those TV shows about singers and theater people have raised expectations super high in our theater department. People think they have to be singing and dancing in perfect synchronization all the time without rehearsal. But real life isn't synchronized like that. It's a mess. Like our theater department.

I open the car door, but I don't get out yet. I turn back to Mom. "You know how I keep telling you that Josh and I are talking? It's a lie," I say.

"Why would you lie about that?"

"I call him, but he never calls me back."

"Never?"

"Like once every six months."

"That makes me angry," Mom says. "I'm going to talk with him."

"Don't," I say. "Let me do it, Mom. I need to have a serious talk with him. I've been avoiding it for too long."

Mom nods. "Good for you," she says.

I get out of the car.

"I'll get a ride home with someone. It might be late."

"How late?"

"Mom, it's a cast party."

"I worry. I can't help it."

"I'll text you before midnight."

"Okay," Mom says, relieved. "Enjoy yourself."

She puts on her signal and pulls out slowly, even though the road is deserted. I open Derek's giant front door and walk into the middle of a wild celebration.

"Welcome to *Fame Lite*," Grace says when she sees me.

"People are excited about the show," I say.

"That's an understatement," Grace says. "You're kind of a hero tonight."

I shrug.

"I'm not trying to get in your pants," Grace says. "Take the compliment."

"Taken," I say.

"Speaking of pants, did you notice I'm out of uniform tonight?" Grace says.

She spins, a cute yellow skirt swirling around her legs. I notice she has a big scab on her knee.

"I've never seen you in a skirt," I say.

"I figured I'd act like a chick for one night. A techie chick."

"Very nice."

"Does it make you want me?" Grace says. She wiggles her eyebrows and I laugh.

"I want you as a friend," I say.

"Do you mean real friends, or the thing where I'm the creepy girl and you're the guy who pretends to like me but you're just putting up with me?"

"Real friends," I say.

Her face lights up.

I catch sight of Reach across the room. He waves.

"What do you think of Reach?" I say.

"He's a jerk."

Across the room, Reach does a robot dance over to an ice bucket filled with soda.

"A strangely compelling jerk," Grace says.

"He's single, you know."

"By the look of things, he's going to stay that way."

"He's a good guy. I mean, once you get past the exterior trappings. Like his personality."

Grace laughs. "Are you trying to pawn me off on your friend?"

"You two might make a good match."

She wrinkles her nose at me.

Reach comes over and hands me a soda from his robot claw. "You made it," he says to me. "And Grace . . ."

He looks down.

". . . in a skirt. Interesting."

"Did you know I have legs?" she says.

"I've seen you walking, so I assumed they were under there somewhere," Reach says.

He glances at her chest.

"I need a soda," Grace says. "I'll let you two have some male-bonding time." She walks into the crowd.

"When did she grow boobs?" Reach says.

"I'm pretty sure she's had them all along."

"Boobs. Legs. I need to take my radar into the shop," Reach says.

"Onto more serious matters," I say.

"Exactly," Reach says. "We need to talk."

We wind our way through the crowd, several techies shouting when they see me and clapping me on the back. Reach and I find a private corner.

"I had a conversation with Johanna," I say.

"That can be an unpleasant experience," Reach says.

"So it's true."

Reach exhales, his long arms slumping by his sides.

"I had a crush on her," he says.

"Had?"

"It's over now. Mostly over. Now I just wince and feel like shit every time I see her."

"Why didn't you tell me?" I say.

"I was embarrassed. I don't even know how it happened. It came out of nowhere. Like Ebola. Horny Ebola."

"We had a pact. No secrets."

"How could I tell you?" Reach says. "She was an actor. I was breaking the techie code."

"In a soft and furry way."

Reach moans and covers his eyes.

"She told you about the teddy bear?" he says.

"At least you didn't do the Altoids tin."

"Half Crack told me I should do the hair-in-the-tin thing, but I never take advice from that guy." He shakes his head like he's trying to get rid of the memory.

"Why didn't you tell me about Summer?" he says.

"Same reason as you."

"We let girls get between us," Reach says.

"Love turns you into a maniac," I say. "There's no other explanation."

"We need a new pact," Reach says. "Friendship first, girlfriends second. A close second. But definitely second."

I raise my soda.

"Here's to getting girlfriends," I say, "so we can put them second."

We tap sodas and drink.

"You really made a tiny Macy's bag?" I say.

"You're not going to let me live that down, are you?"

"Not for at least six months."

I hear girls laughing down the hall. I scan the room, trying to locate Summer.

"What are you going to do about your own actor problem?" Reach says.

"What do you think?"

"Are you asking for my advice?"

"I guess I am. Imagine that."

"I think you should grow a pair," Reach says. "Actually, I saw you out on that stage tonight. You already have a pair. A big pair. You just need to swing them a little bit."

"It could get embarrassing," I say.

"We're techies. Embarrassment is like mother's milk to us."

"In that case, I'm going to take a walk," I say.

"Try the living room," Reach says. "And hey—I've got your back."

"I'm glad," I say.

I throw him a salute and step into the crowd.

As I walk through the house, I'm surprised to find things divided just like they always were. There are actor rooms and a techie rooms, actor conversations and techie conversations. Part of me thought that tonight's show would bring everyone together in a new way. But it feels like people left the show and went right back to business as usual.

I find Summer in the living room like Reach predicted. The whole theater department is in here, divided like Germany after World War II, techies on one side and actors on the other.

I walk through the techies. They seem excited to see me, maybe a little surprised, too. I'm not exactly known for my social "A" game. I shake hands as I go and I'm friendly to everyone, but I don't stop walking.

I pause when I get to the dividing line between techies and actors.

That's when I see Derek.

He's deep in actor territory, talking to a large group and gesticulating. I can imagine what he's been saying about me.

I ruined his show. I did it on purpose. I don't care about the theater, only about my career.

Who knows what else?

Summer isn't in his group. She's all the way on the far side of the room near the unlit fireplace.

I head towards her. There are some actors in my way, and I excuse myself. I'm almost there when Derek appears in front of me, blocking the way.

He smiles like he's happy to see me.

"Welcome to my humble abode," he says, and he sweeps his arm in a circle around the gargantuan living room.

"You mean your dad's abode," I say.

He shrugs.

"He built the house. But he's out of town, so we all get to enjoy it," he says.

"I thought he was coming to the show," I say.

"I thought so, too," Derek says.

Derek looks sad, and for a second I feel sorry for him. But then he starts smiling again.

"It's not a problem," he says. "In fact it worked out better for me."

"What do you mean?"

"If my father had been here, he wouldn't have seen my show. He would have seen your giant candelabra. By the time he gets back next weekend, we will be up and running, tech and all. Then he can see the real thing."

Derek laughs to himself.

"Yes, indeed," he says. "Tonight was exciting, but next weekend is going to be groundbreaking."

He steps back and puts his arm around Summer.

"Lots to celebrate," he says.

It's not like Summer melts into his arms. Far from it. But she doesn't shrug him off either. I can see where this is headed. I'm out of the picture now. He'll pick up where he left off with his design, with Summer. It's his theater department again. He'll go until he gets what he wants or until he's bored.

The thought is almost too much for me.

I want to run away. Maybe Mom is still outside, and I can get a ride home with her. Maybe nobody will remember that I was here.

But I've spent my life running from moments like this.

"I want to talk to Summer," I say.

Derek's eyes widen in surprise.

"But does she want to talk to you?" he says.

There's one way to find out.

"Hi," I say to Summer.

"Hi," she says.

The room quiets down. I can feel the actors and techies behind me, watching.

"I don't want to be the funny friend," I say.

"What's the funny friend?" Summer says.

"You know, the guy who hangs around you, and you tell him all your secrets or whatever, and then he smells like your shampoo."

"What are you talking about, Ziggy?"

"I don't want to be just friends."

"Who do you want to be?" Derek says. His arm is still around her shoulders.

"I want to be more than that," I say to Summer.

I feel my face burning.

"I don't understand," Summer says.

"I'm trying to tell you that you're special," I say.

"She knows that already," Derek says.

"Maybe I don't know it," Summer says. "Maybe I want to hear it."

"Yawn," Derek says.

"Tell me more," Summer says.

Derek looks pissed. He takes his arm off her shoulder.

"Give it your best shot," he says to me.

"First of all, you're pretty," I say. "And cool. And funny. And pretty."

"Ziggy, I have to be honest. You're kind of laming out here," she says.

"Please be quiet for a second," I say.

"Tell her to shut up," Derek says. "Smart move."

"Why should I be quiet?" Summer says.

"Because I'm trying to tell you something important," I say.

She takes a breath and waits.

"I'm so bad at this," I say.

"You're doing pretty good now," she says.

"I like you a lot," I say.

"In a friend way?" she says.

"In a girlfriend way."

She looks into my eyes.

I'm used to actors looking over my shoulder, looking past me, looking straight through. That's not what Summer does. Not now.

"Well, Ziggy. That's something to say."

"It sure is," Derek says. "A little cliché. Not at all poetic."

"I'm a techie. I'm not good with poetry. I'm better with the real thing."

"Is this the real thing?" she says.

"I'm pretty sure it is."

"I think . . . ," she says.

And then she pauses, biting her lip with her right front tooth. I see the little line there, the scar from the accident she had when she was a kid. I wish I had been there when Summer fell. I would have put my arms around her and hugged her until she stopped crying.

"I think . . . ," she says again.

"What?" I say softly, because I can see she's struggling with something.

"I think it's good news, what you said."

"Why is that?" I say.

"Because I like you, too," she says.

"Theater people care about each other," Derek says. "It's natural to be friends."

"As more than a friend," Summer says. "As a boyfriend."

Derek's smile goes away.

"You two are creeping me out," he says.

He looks across the room at the group of actresses who play the fairies. There's a new girl there. A freshman.

"Cheers, ladies," he calls out, and heads towards them.

"Thank God," Summer says. "I thought he'd never leave."

"You don't like him?"

"I mean he's talented and all. But a little bit of arrogant Brit goes a long way," she says. "Anyway, he's just jealous."

"Of what?"

"Of you. Of what a star you were tonight."

"Do you think so?" I say.

"I was impressed," Summer says.

I glance behind me. Reach and Grace are standing across the room watching us. They both give me the thumbs-up at the same time.

"To tell you the truth, I'm surprised you want to talk to me at all," Summer says.

"Why?"

"You were pretty angry in the practice room."

"You were acting like a jerk," I say.

"I know. I deserved it. That was stupid of me."

"Very stupid."

"Ouch, Ziggy."

"What happened? You totally changed overnight."

"I freaked out. Derek was telling me things, the actors were talking behind my back—add that to the pressure of the show opening, and I kind of went crazy."

"Are you going to go crazy again?"

"I don't plan on it," she says.

Just then a song starts to play. A love song from the musical *West Side Story*. A giant *whoop* lets go from the actors in the room.

"What about your *just friends* speech?" I say.

"I don't want to be just friends. That would be terrible," Summer says.

A bunch of actors jump up and start doing dance moves. Soon actors are spinning around us, singing the lyrics as loud as they can, doing fakey vibrato and loving every minute of it.

"I think we should dance," Summer says.

"Slight problem. I don't know how," I say.

"Put your arms around me," she says.

I wrap my arms around her back, and she pulls me in close. I smell the delicious Summer smell.

"Hold me tighter," she says.

And I do. We stand in the middle of the party, our arms around each other. There are some weird looks from the actors in the room, but some smiles, too. Most of the techies are smiling.

"What now?" I whisper.

"We have sex," she says.

"Really?"

"Ziggy! Are you serious?"

"I don't know these things!"

She gives me a playful punch on the arm, then pulls me towards her.

"Just rock back and forth," she says in my ear.

We sway in each other's arms, barely moving as people dance around us.

I think about my dad. I wish he could see me like this. I start to get the empty feeling inside, so I hug her tighter. The feeling doesn't go away. It just gets softer, like I can feel it and still be okay.

"How do you feel?" Summer says.

"Like I'm waking up from a terrible dream," I say.

Summer pulls me close.

"Wake up, wake up," she says. "I'm right here."

I think about what the cast party would look like from the catwalk. People's heads bobbing up and down, moving closer and farther apart. Music heard from above. Fun viewed from up high and far away.

I'm not sure yet, but I think it's better down here.